'...generous and closely observed stories ...ely alert to the details of human behaviour... ...drilling into those who live the most or...

Sydney Morning ...

By the same author

The Aerodynamics of Pork
Ease
Kansas in August
Facing the Tank
Little Bits of Baby
The Cat Sanctuary
Caesar's Wife
The Facts of Life
Dangerous Pleasures
Tree Surgery for Beginners
Rough Music
A Sweet Obscurity
Friendly Fire
Notes from the Exhibition
The Whole Day Through

'...much alive'

...proves that the short story is...
Daily Express

'Vivid, believable characters ... [Gale] suddenly twists a sunny tale into the macabre, to end on an uneasy note. Gale has a light touch with social commentary but the undertones are often menacing'
Times Literary Supplement

PATRICK GALE was born on
spent his infancy at Wands
governed, then grew up in
farm near Land's End. His
from an Exhibition and *Th*

To learn more please visit v

From the reviews of *Gentle*

'Dark, witty and often obli
of difficult fathers and ga
random or deliberate acts of
power and the lack of it a
in unexpected ways, offeri
certain and where love or its
CA

'A selection of succulent titl
showcase his capacity for
macabre sense of humour w
human feeling'

'Provides further evidence of
and wonderfully eclectic ran

'Gale has a distinctive sense o
for something sinister to be l
unruffled and genteel surface
enjoyable collection which
still very much

'Intelligen
is exquisit
at his bes
lives'

PATRICK GALE

Gentleman's Relish

FOURTH ESTATE · *London*

Fourth Estate
An imprint of HarperCollins*Publishers*
77–85 Fulham Palace Road
Hammersmith
London W6 8JB
www.4thestate.co.uk

Visit our authors' blog at www.fifthestate.co.uk
Love this book? www.bookarmy.com

This Fourth Estate paperback edition published 2010
1

First published in Great Britain by Fourth Estate in 2009

A catalogue record for this book is available from the British Library

ISBN 978-0-00-731346-4

Set in Sabon by
Palimpsest Book Production Limited,
Grangemouth, Stirlingshire

Printed and bound in Great Britain by Clays Ltd, St Ives plc

Mixed Sources

Product group from well-managed
forests and other controlled sources
www.fsc.org Cert no. SW-COC-001806
© 1996 Forest Stewardship Council

FSC is a non-profit international organisation established to promote the
responsible management of the world's forests. Products carrying the FSC label
are independently certified to assure consumers that they come from forests that
are managed to meet the social, economic and ecological needs of present and
future generations.

Find out more about HarperCollins and the environment at
www.harpercollins.co.uk/green

For Aidan Hicks

CONTENTS

THE LESSON

Jane stepped outside with a basket of washing and her hair was whipped about her face. Even in June, theirs was one of the windiest gardens she had known. Shortly after moving there she had invested in an extra set of pegs; laundry had to be doubly secured if she wasn't to be forever retrieving pillowslips from rosebushes and rewashing shirts the wind had rolled around flowerbeds. It was a miracle there *were* flowerbeds, let alone that she could persuade much to grow in them. Lavender thrived, and rosemary and a kind of low, blue-flowered tree lupin whose seed a cousin had sent up from Cornwall. But the only roses that could cope with the near-constant wind and occasional salt spray were tough, rugosa hybrids, more leaf than flower, and she had abandoned all hope of recreating the lush beds of Stanwell Perpetual and Etoile de Hollande she had relished at Camp Hill and Liverpool.

The sheets cracked like circus whips as she battled to hang them out. She had heard of governors' wives who cheerfully entrusted everything but smalls to the prison laundries but she had never cared to do that; it would have been a step too far into institutional life. Besides, she needed occupation. With both children away in boarding school – at her parents' expense – her days were all too long and solitary.

She had learned by degrees that marriage to a prison governor was not unlike marriage to a priest, only without the flower arranging or the constant invasion of the family home. As with priests, one lived on the job and the job came first. Her husband left her after an early breakfast then remained in the prison until he returned to her, invariably pallid with exhaustion, minutes before supper was ready. And it was a rare weekend when she did not have to share him with the men at least once a day.

He called them that: *The Men*. They only became *prisoners* if they escaped, and there had been no successful breakouts from this prison in years. On one end of a rocky promontory jutting out from the coast, it had started life as a small fortress in Henry VIII's time, and had then been greatly expanded under threat of Napoleonic invasion.

The prison dated from the 1840s and made use of the enormously thick fortress walls and the ferocious cliffs on the site's two seaward sides. The Governor's House, also early Victorian, was severely elegant. Both were built from slabs of the local stone – prized by town councils the world over – which the prisoners continued to hew from the quarries that hemmed the prison in on its landward side.

Even more than at Liverpool, and far more than on the Isle of Wight, she felt herself imprisoned there. She no longer had the children as an excuse for excursions. The only other women nearby were officers' wives and, even had she wanted to, it was not done to befriend them and risk showing favouritism. At each of her husband's previous, five-yearly postings, she had socialized with the chaplain's wife – in one case making a cherished friend whose comfortingly spiky conversation she missed acutely – but here the chaplain was acidly single, his house kept by a savage widowed sister Jane encountered as little as good manners would allow.

There was nothing to stop her making day trips but she had yet to acquire the habit of enjoying culture or walks on her own and was inhibited by the brutal landscape that lay between the prison and anything of interest.

Her mother had been a governor's wife too and, like many of her tribe, an army wife before that.

She thrived on the predominant maleness of the prison environment, enjoyed the sense of her extravagant femininity in such a setting as her little car was waved through by the guards or her skinny legs were ogled by a working party in her garden.

By contrast Jane had always found that being the lone woman on an island of masculinity made her yearn after invisibility. She had dreams of anonymous city life in which she walked streets so bustling with women, all of them better dressed and longer-legged than her, that she felt herself blissfully eclipsed.

She peered down from one end of the washing line to the heavily supervised road that wound down towards the outer gates. A troop of men was being marched out to work in the quarries. Their voices reached her, noisy with wisecracks and bravado. Her husband claimed they liked the quarry work, which Jane found hard to believe, but certainly they seemed to approach each shift with good spirits. Perhaps it was the sea air they relished and exercise in the sunshine instead of the boarding-school gases of the prison meals her husband insisted on sharing or the medieval stink of the cell blocks at slopping-out time.

One of the men looked up at her then nudged his mate and pointed. She stepped back behind the flapping sheets as the whistling started. The sheets were almost dry already. On some days the washing had become quite stiff by the time she fetched it in.

'Ma'am?'

She turned, startled. An officer was waiting at the garden gate. He had one of the men with him. An older man. Handsome. Respectable-looking.

'Yes?' she asked, unconsciously holding the peg bag to her front as she approached them.

The officer doffed his hat and she recognized him from the Knobbly Knees competition at the Christmas party. 'Governor said you needed some bookshelves making. We thought Glossop, here, could make them for you.'

'Are you a joiner, Glossop?' she asked.

'I trained as a cabinetmaker, ma'am.'

'Excellent. Let me show you what we're after.'

Seen closer to, Glossop was younger than she thought: her husband's age, only prematurely aged by prison. His eyes were the colour of English sea, his dark hair silvered at his temples.

Along with the house and unlimited heating and hot water, one of the perks of the job was the regular availability of trusties – many of them with valuable trades – to help around the place. Over the years she had seen roses pruned, lawns edged, rooms plastered and painted, sash windows repaired, even silk lampshades made by men eager to break the monotony of prison routine by exercising old skills. Apart from the shopkeepers who delivered provisions from what

7

she thought of as *The Mainland,* the only trades-man she ever had to pay herself throughout her marriage was her hairdresser.

Now that her son was away at school and showing every sign of becoming as keen a reader as his father, she wanted to replace his rather babyish painted bookcase with something larger and more adult that would be a pleasant surprise for him on his return.

Glossop took measurements and scribbled them on a pad while the officer stood by.

'Seven shelves, do you reckon?' he asked. 'Or six with a larger one at the bottom?'

'Six with a larger one,' she said.

'And how about a nice cornice at the top?'

'A cornice?'

'Like on that lovely bureau bookcase on the landing.'

'Well that would be lovely.' She was startled that he had noticed her antiques and automatically wondered if he had been a burglar.

'And a sort of skirting board to match what you've already got in here?'

'You could do that?'

'I could.' Glossop smiled, at which the officer's expression grew yet more wintry.

'Then yes please.'

'I can't do you mahogany, like out there.'

'No. Of course not. Pine, I suppose.'

'Or oak. We've got plenty of oak at the moment.'

'Have you?'

'Glossop has been making new pews for the chapel, ma'am.'

'I must go and see. Oak would be much better than pine. It ages so nicely. When could you start?'

Glossop glanced at the officer. 'I could measure and cut the shelves and framework this afternoon,' he said cautiously. 'Make the joints. I could bring them in and start fitting them together in here same time tomorrow.'

'That would be lovely. Thank you.'

Invariably she found she was too friendly, even gushing, when talking to the men, which she never was with officers. She supposed she felt sorry for them. Sorry and rather afraid.

'Is that yours?' he asked as they turned to go, pointing at the fishing rod propped in a corner.

'No. It's my boy's. His godmother gave it to him and he never uses it.'

'Shame,' Glossop said. 'That would make a nice little spinning rod.' And the officer led him away.

As she closed the door behind them, she noticed he had left behind him a trace of the prisoner's habitual smell – an entirely male tang; a blend of cheap tobacco, under-washed clothing and confined body. It was a smell she found penetrated her husband's tweed jackets but never his person.

That afternoon she rang her husband on the

internal telephone and asked if she could visit the prison chapel to inspect Glossop's handiwork. He was too busy with interviews to take her himself but he sent an officer to escort her.

Most of the pews were just as she had remembered from the last carol service: the worst kind of late nineteenth century pitch pine, dull, dark and penitential, deliberately cut too short in the seat for slouching. Glossop's pews – he had made four – were far paler, made of simply waxed oak. He had felt obliged to echo the silhouette of the others but his furniture was lightened by small details. A fine moulding along the seat edge and the back was just made for one's thumbs to fiddle with during hymns and sermons. On the length of the little retaining shelf designed to hold hymnals and prayer books he had carved a sequence of birds. They were all local ones, clearly identifiable, the sort the more observant men must spot all the time – cormorant, shag, herring gull, jackdaw; toughened, cliff-top birds for a tough, cliff-top prison.

'Aren't they lovely?' she exclaimed, charmed, but the officer would not be drawn beyond a 'Very nice, ma'am.'

'What did he do?' she asked her husband over dinner.

'Glossop? You know it's much better if you don't know. He's a trusty, though. Quite harmless. You'll be perfectly safe.'

10

'I wasn't worried. Just curious. Cheese or fruit?'

When Glossop returned the following day, bringing his tools and wood with him on a trolley, she encouraged the officer who had escorted him to leave them alone together. 'It's quite all right,' she said, when he hesitated. 'I'll ring when Glossop's ready to leave.'

It was impossible to tell if Glossop appreciated the gesture or not. He simply concentrated on bringing his things up the stairs and carefully spread a spotless dustsheet over the bedroom carpet. She offered him the radio but he gently declined and she realized that if there was any pleasure for him in this assignment, it lay in the brief luxury of peace and quiet, of being amidst muffling surfaces – wood, carpets and curtains – after the cold clangour of metal doors, metal walkways, metal plates and metal mugs. She made them both proper coffee – in a pot – and set a tray with china mugs and a plate with chocolate biscuits and rock cakes on it – far more than she would offer should the acid chaplain come to call.

He didn't seem to mind her watching him work – perhaps he appreciated feminine company, even a middle-aged housewife's – and he answered all her questions, about wood and tools and how he learnt his trade from his father but had taught himself to carve since imprisonment to give his hands occupation.

'Must get lonely for you, living out here,' he said at last, as he was checking the angle of a shelf with his spirit level.

'Sorry,' she said. 'Am I talking too much? Sometimes people visit, real people. Sorry. That sounded awful. But you know what I mean. And I think I gabble at them like a thing possessed . . . Yes,' she admitted at last, when he had let her foolish, rambling answer wither on the air. 'It does get lonely. With the children both away and my husband at . . . at work and no friends nearer than a day's drive away. I like my own company but not here. Not much. It's oppressive.'

'I think it's meant to be,' he said drily. 'Why not go for walks?'

'Oh I used to. But then our dog got old and died and, with the children not here, I didn't have the energy to train another puppy.'

'You should go fishing.'

'Fishing?' The idea was absurd. She pictured herself, mannish in tweeds and waders. 'Oh I'm sure it's terribly complicated and I wouldn't know how and anyway, the nearest rivers are . . .' She realized she had no idea where the nearest angling rivers were and tried to remember where she and the departed dog had last come upon anglers at their intently private business.

'Rod like that and the right sort of float, you wouldn't need a river. You could fish for bass.'

'In the sea?'

'Off a rock.'

She thought of the bass her brother had presented her with last time they stayed with him, of its sweet white flesh, and its skin deliciously crisped with a rubbing of soy sauce before grilling. 'Oh,' she demurred. 'It's my boy's rod . . .'

But her son had barely touched the rod – a present designed to lure his head out of books – and she knew he'd be only relieved to see it get some use.

'I wouldn't know where to begin,' she said, staring at it.

'It's easy,' he said. 'If you're patient and you're not squeamish. It was my mother taught me. You might want gardening gloves, for when you come to handle the scales. The fins can be sharp as any rose thorn.'

Impulsively she took the rod from its corner and held it out to him. 'Show me,' she said.

'Are you left-handed,' he asked, 'or right?'

Standing closer than was probably appropriate, so that she could smell the sweat and wood shavings on him, and guiding her hands with his, he showed her how to hold the rod, how to cast, how the winder thing worked and how to prevent it spinning the line into an impossible tangle at the moment of casting.

While she blushed furiously, he raided her son's little fishing satchel (simultaneous gift of a second

13

godparent carefully briefed by the first) and assembled float, tiny plastic balls and a hook for her and tied them on along with a tiny length of rubber band he called her *stop*. He showed her how to adjust the stop until the float hung vertically in the water. He showed her how she could carefully secure the hook to part of the rod then tighten the line so that she had everything in place for fishing and would need less to carry. He showed her on her Dorset road map how to find the rocks where he had often caught bass when the tide was on the turn and he told her where in Weymouth to buy little packets of sand eels to use as bait. He wrote the name and address in tidy script with his stump of carpenter's pencil.

'Just tell him I sent you,' he said. 'And he'll give you good service. He knows me. We were in the war together.'

At first she had been humouring him, merely being politely curious, but he took the matter so in earnest she found herself swept up in it. And as he described where to park the car on the coast road and how to find the discreet footpath that led to his favoured fishing rocks, she could see what it was costing him to picture a loved place he could no longer visit. She felt shamed into following his instructions to the letter.

As Glossop had suggested, she spent an hour practising casting on the windswept lawn, far from

14

any bushes, until she was fairly confident. Then she went fishing. She didn't tell her husband. Eccentricity unsettled him. Besides, he showed little curiosity as to how she spent her days so long as she wasn't spending money.

She felt some doubt about presenting herself at the angling shop as an acquaintance of a criminal in case she was unwittingly passing on a coded message to an accomplice but the name worked like a charm and the weather-beaten man behind the counter was at once all affability and helpfulness, checking over her kit to ensure she had all she needed for the task in hand and adding a ladylike little club called a *priest* to her armoury. When he explained what it was for she realized she had always pictured fish as somehow dying of defeat, in effect, within moments of being landed and the man saw her doubt.

'One quick tap on the back of the head does the trick,' he told her. 'If it's a mackerel, you don't even need the priest – just stick a finger in his mouth and click the head back, like this.' He mimed the swift, deadly gesture and made a soft, crunching noise as he did so.

On her first trip to Glossop's fishing spot she caught nothing, although something took sly bites off the part of her sand eels that dangled free of the hook. She did not mind, though, since there was intense pleasure to be had simply from standing still on a flat rock so near the surface of the sea, where she could admire the acrobatics of seabirds and commune with the doggy faces of the seals that bobbed up to watch her.

She reported back to Glossop in detail as he rubbed beeswax into wood. His questions taxed her powers of recall. What direction was the current moving? Was there much weed? How far from the rock was her float landing? How good was visibility through the water below her? And how far off were the gannets feeding?

Awareness sharpened by his keen questioning, she returned two days later, at the time of morning when much perusal of a tide table told him the water movements would be ideal for bass.

She caught something almost at once. It was big. She could see it fighting the line in the water. In her excitement she forgot which way to wind the winder and which way its little levers should be flicked. She paid line out when she meant to reel it in. She snagged the line on a rock. She was entirely unprepared for the way rod and line seemed to stretch and bend to the point where her frantic winding seemed to take almost no effect. Then, with a lunging and tugging that was surely as incorrect as it was ungraceful, she managed to land the beast.

Even to her eye, trained solely by a lifetime of fishmongers' slabs and a few evenings of poring over *The Observer's Book of Sea Fishes*, she knew

16

it wasn't a bass. But it *was* beautiful, covered in a violent pattern of turquoise and dull gold and with thick, gasping lips of sky-blue. It was hard to believe something so glamorous could come from such unexotically British waters. She was quite unready for the way its eye met hers, rolling, desperate, or for the violence of its thrashing when her hands drew near, or the threatening spikes of its dorsal fin.

She couldn't kill it. Not possibly. She ignored the priest, tugged on the clumsy gardening gloves and, fighting the urge to cry out in distress, held it firmly down while she tried to free the hook from its mouth. This was not a thing she had discussed with Glossop. They'd talked only in terms of hunter and prey, not of captor and release. After what felt like minutes of the poor thing drowning in air, she worked out for herself that the hook's barb meant it had to be drawn through in the direction it was already travelling. She took her little pen knife, fumbled off the gloves to open it, got the gloves back on, almost lost the knife into a rock pool, cut the line, teased the hook out through the creature's jaw – which produced no blood, she thanked God, or she'd have surely given up – then tossed it back into the water.

For a few dreadful seconds she thought she had killed it, as it merely hung in the water and began to turn its pale belly to the sky, a plump offering for gulls. Then it shook itself and flew down into the shadows beneath the rock.

'Sounds like a wrasse,' Glossop told her. 'Corkwing Wrasse. A proper sport fish. You're blooded now. No stopping you!'

She looked *wrasse* up in her cookery books and was relieved to find it described as having watery, rather yellow flesh, fit only for Portuguese stews. Its Latin name, aptly enough it seemed, was *turdus*.

Glossop went on to make shelves for her daughter's room and two bedside tables for her own, then, without warning, was deprived of trusty status halfway through making her a cheese board.

'An act of violence,' was the only explanation her husband offered, and he took against the bedside tables and banished them to the spare room, claiming his had a wobble.

After several more wrasse and a dispiriting quantity of mackerel, which at least taught her how to kill unflinchingly, she landed her first bass later that summer and fed it to him, steamed, *à la Chinoise*. She would have liked to cook it for Glossop but, of course, that was out of the question. Instead she bought him an oceanographic map of the Dorset coast and posted it to him from Weymouth, along with a postcard of swans at Abbotsbury.

Success at last! she wrote. *Only 2½ pounds but delicious and so satisfying. First of many, I hope. Thank you so much*. She hesitated over how to close, aware of rules, aware that a prison cell was all too public and that letters went astray. She used *Yours sincerely, Mrs Whiteley* correctly then defiantly gave him her Christian name, in brackets, and added a ps – *I shall guard your rock for you* – knowing it would mean nothing to anyone else.

Jane became rather an expert at sea angling and bought much and varied tackle from Glossop's army friend in Weymouth but her husband's next posting was a landlocked one. The new house's lush and sheltered rose beds were no compensation.

COOKERY

A favourite piece of broodily autumnal Fauré came on the radio. Perry turned it up and sang along under his breath, still unused to the delight of having the house to himself and being able to make as much noise as he liked. He lifted a saucepan lid to check on the leeks which were sweating in a pool of butter. He prodded them with a wooden spoon then turned off the heat, ground in some pepper and grated in some nutmeg. Nutmeg subtly sweetened the taste and blended nicely with the air of slightly burnt butter. One had to be sparing, however; too much, and the spice overcame the taste of leek rather than merely enhancing it.

He continued singing to himself as he whisked in eggs, cream and some crumbled Wensleydale cheese. Swathing his hands in a towel, he pulled a baking tray from the oven on which two small tart cases had been baking blind under a shroud of silicone parchment weighted with earthenware beans. They were done to perfection; dry without being coloured yet. He allowed the steam to escape from them then, biting his lower lip from the fear of them breaking, tipped each of them gently onto the palm of his hand then slid them, naked, back to the baking tray. He spooned the leek mixture in, sprinkled on a few Parmesan shavings then returned the tray to the oven and set the timer.

The cat, Edie, was clawing at the window and, being on the large side due to a diet of culinary leavings and field mice, threatening to dislodge the herbs that grew on the sill. Perry let her in, kissed her nose in greeting and set her down a saucer of cream. She was the only cat he had known to purr and eat at the same time. The sound was faintly indecent and spoke of appetites beyond the power of man to tame.

'Cookery is power,' his mother told him at an early age. She meant it jokingly. Minutes before, she had taught him how to make a simple chocolate toffee sauce to pour over ice cream (butter, sugar, cocoa, a few grains of instant coffee – he made it occasionally still) and was laughing at how instant a reaction it won with some schoolfriends he brought home to lunch.

He had little sense of humour at that age, even

less than he had now, and he asked her, quite solemnly, what she meant.

'I'll tell you when we're alone,' she said, and winked.

He asked her again that night, while he sat on the end of her bed and watched her, fascinated, as she teased out her dancing hair in the breeze from the hair drier. She was taken aback at his earnestness. She had forgotten both sauce and comment. He had thought of little else all day.

'Men have very simple needs,' she said, 'sleep, food, warmth and the other thing. But hunger is the most powerful. When your stomach's turning in on itself, you can't concentrate. When you eat something delicious, you're happy, you're grateful. A griddle's more potent than any gun, Perry.' She laughed. 'Why frighten people into doing what you want when you can win their love with cake? That hubble-bubble stuff in *Macbeth* is a parody of a recipe; a cauldron's just an oversized casserole, after all. If you ask me, those women they burned at the stake were simply cooks who led whole communities by the nose and tongue.'

With the untutored taste buds of childhood, he had favoured sweet recipes at first. Happily these tended to be those involving the most magical transformations. Thus his early cookery lessons carried all the attraction of games with a chemistry set. There was that hot chocolate sauce that, once he had learned to let it boil sufficiently, set into filling-tugging caramel on contact with ice cream. There was the sequence of hot desserts, nicknamed *chemical puddings* by his mother, in which an unpromising sludge would rise up through a watery layer during baking, thickening it into a rich sauce as it formed a puffily cakey crust above it. Victoria sponge taught him pride. Patience he learned through meringue; those wrist-numbing extra minutes of whisking that divided egg whites that were merely stiff from those that were said to be *standing in peaks*, and the slow baking in a cool oven which managed mysteriously to produce a confection so crumbly and dry. It was only with chocolate brownies, however, with which a girlfriend's older brother was so easily persuaded to drop his jeans for a five-minute *scientific* inspection, that Perry learned the extent of his new-found power.

Adult, savoury cookery was taught piecemeal, largely through being asked to help out with occasional tasks. Learning how to brown chicken thighs, roll pieces of steak in seasoned flour, dissect and meticulously de-seed red peppers, he combined his new techniques with what he saw his mother doing and so added *coq au vin*, *boeuf en daube* and *ratatouille* to a still succinct repertoire.

'If you can cook,' she told him, 'you'll never be hungry, but if you can cook *well*, if you can do more than just feed people, you'll be popular too. You'll be able to choose who likes you.'

Thrilled by the potency of such a spell, for he was a scrawny child who had yet to grow into his nose, he hung on her every word. He followed her about the garden absorbing wisdom.

'Parsley,' she pronounced. 'Useful but common. The curly one is only really usable in sauce and soup. And never use the flat-leaved one unthinkingly. Often this plant, chervil, will do much better. Taste it. Go on. See? Now try this. Coriander. Superb stuff. You can use it almost like a vegetable, by the handful, but be careful again. Used in the wrong context it tastes like soap and it sticks to teeth as embarrassingly as spinach.'

In season, she led him around the fields and lanes behind the house introducing him to blackberries, sloes, elder bushes, mushrooms, crab apples, sorrel.

When Perry turned ten, shortly after his creation of a puffball and bacon roulade had seduced a new neighbour and demoralized the neighbour's wife, his mother fell ill. For a few weeks, without anyone's appearing to notice, he inherited her apron, and whisked up menu after comforting menu for his father and older brothers, reading cookery books in bed and skiving off afternoon sports sessions at school to race into town on his bicycle before the covered market closed. When she returned, grey and shattered after her operation, she was grateful to have had her wooden spoon usurped, still more to taste his nutritious soups and cunning vegetables after two weeks of hospital pap.

Her gratitude, however, seemed to break the peaceful spell of his father's quiescence. It was as though he were noticing for the first time as Perry stirred his sauces and deftly shredded roots and nuts, swamped in a practical but undeniably floral apron.

'Why don't you play rugby like Geoff?' he asked. 'You'd like rugby. Once you got used to it.'

'Sport bores me. What do you think of this duck? Was the fennel a mistake? Maybe celeriac would work better, or even parsnip. If I could get it to caramelize properly without the skin burning . . .'

Perry was duly banished to a boarding school on the Yorkshire coast, handpicked for its bracingly sporty philosophy and lack of opportunities for any science more domestic than the use of Ralgex and Universal Embrocation. His mother was brought down from her sickbed and set back to work at the kitchen stove. She collapsed there shortly afterwards and died of an internal haemorrhage halfway through assembling a deceptively humble fish pie. Perry cursed his father for his cruelty but laid on a suitable buffet for her funeral and brought his seduction of the neighbour to an electric conclusion with the aid of some witty yet somehow mournful filo parcels of pigeon, leek and sultana.

He hated school and counted off the passing weeks like a prisoner. His impatience to be free had more to do with the liberty to have access to more inspiring ingredients than with any brutalities visited on him. His growing mastery over food continued to protect him like a hero's winged sandals or magic armour. An ability to dress crab and whip up a mayonnaise won him an entrée to the shielding comforts of the prefects' common room in his second week and the older boys soon set him to baking them cakes instead of forcing him out onto icy playing fields. He even came to look forward to overnight field trips with the cadet corps, given charge as he was of the campfire kitchen. Since adolescents have always lurched between the kindred demands of belly and groin, cookery also brought him sporadic tastes of rough-handed romance.

His father and brothers had long dismissed him as effetely artistic and were as surprised as he was when he began to specialize in chemistry. Boarding school had given him a taste for independence. Without his mother there, the family home held little appeal for him and while passing through university and qualifying as a forensic scientist, he went there as little as possible. (He made exceptions for his brothers' successive weddings, miserable occasions where the poor quality of the catering made him more than usually grateful that he had kept cookery as a vice and not pursued it as a livelihood.)

He had only the one live-in lover, first encountered in the meat aisle of a local supermarket. Douglas had come out shopping in tennis clothes, fresh, or rather not, from a match. Perry could not help noticing the way the chilled air from the meat cabinets raised goose bumps on his legs and Douglas noticed him notice. After smiling, smirking then grinning encounters beside toiletries, Kosher and home baking successively, the evening had ended in Perry cooking Douglas lamb noisettes in a pink peppercorn sauce. Smug and yawning twelve hours later, he made them scrambled eggs and bacon. It took only two more dinners for Douglas to move in.

It was a love expressed as Perry knew best, in generous helpings, judiciously seasoned. Over four years, Douglas added running and secret dieting to tennis as he fought in vain the extra poundage that Perry's devotion was heaping on him. Then he fell ill and for three years after that, Perry became an expert in nutritional coaxing as he tried in vain to stave off Douglas's inexorable spells of weight loss, vanished appetite or nausea. The most innocent foods – yoghurt, bread, cheese – would suddenly be branded as enemies. His ingenuity was stretched to the limit. Whenever Douglas was in hospital, Perry would cook a portable supper for them both and make a point of their still sharing an evening meal there, even if Douglas could manage no more than a spoonful before sinking back on the pillows in defeat. Never had the preparation of food carried such an emotional charge for him.

Douglas's was the second funeral feast he had cooked, beating tears into cake batter, anger into cream. He intended it to be his last.

After Douglas there had been men occasionally, but no more lovers. Perry's experience of desire had always been so bound up in the pleasures of the table that he found it hard to surrender for long to any romance that was not essentially domestic. Then the hole in his domestic routine was unexpectedly filled.

A stroke after a hip operation left his father incapacitated. There was a gruesome council of war in which the brothers, abetted by child-worn wives, agreed that residential homes were both soulless and ruinously expensive. Perry had room in his house. Perry had experience of home nursing thanks to his 'lodger's' long illness. They would each pay a nominal monthly sum to their younger brother and he should take their father in. He had never declared his sexuality, assuming it would be taken as read and, as they confronted him with their tidy plan, he sensed it was too late to do so now. He had allowed them to assume he was merely a bachelor, a eunuch with a way with sauces. He had allowed them to assume that, for all their initial doubts, his work for CID meant that he had been vetted as 'sound'. Playing hard to define, he had played into their hands. He could hardly turn around and complain that visiting a speechless, incontinent, not to say unmusical parent on him would starve a love life that was already gasping for sustenance.

At first it seemed like an abominable invasion of his privacy. The old man might have lost control of tongue and bladder but retained his bullying nature and store of indignation. Gradually, however, Perry saw that there was no cause for fear. He was in charge now. He decided what the old man could and could not eat, when he would bathe, when he could watch television and, indeed, what he would watch. To cover the long hours he spent at work in the police laboratories, he took pleasure in hiring just the sort of camp, Irish nurse his father would loathe. Said treasure wore a uniform he described as Doris Blue. He was delighted when Perry confided that his father had been sleeping with men on the sly all his married life and was a wicked old flirt with wandering hands. Perry often came home to find the two of them watching films in which men loved men or women tap-danced and sang their hearts out. The nurse would be watching, at least, and singing along where appropriate. Perry's father would be merely staring, aghast, in the direction in which he had been so mercilessly wedged with scatter cushions.

Perry opened them an account at a specialist

video library. In twelve months his father was exposed to the entire output of Crawford, Davis, Stanwyck, Garland, and the Turners Kathleen and Lana. He became a passive expert on the complete weepies of Douglas Sirk – of which the nurse was especially fond – and even the most misbegotten of MGM's musical output. He sat, breathing heavily, through any film that could be remotely described as lesbian or gay, subtitles, Kenneth Anger and all. He watched nothing pornographic, however, at least nothing hard core. Despite Perry's bland assurances, the nurse was sure the excitement would have dire effects on his bladder or even his heart.

It startled Perry to find that he could be so vindictive. Apart from some singularly unhelpful grief counselling after Douglas died, he had never been in therapy and was not given to self-analysis. He had never given voice to the damage his father had done him, so had never given it substance. Even now, he did not immediately seek a retributive justification for what he was doing.

He did not abuse his father physically, although the odd smack might have seemed only the mild repayment of a long-outstanding debt. He dressed him. He undressed him. He bathed him. He changed his incontinence pads. If he spoon-fed him the kind of food his father had always dismissed as foreign or *nancy*, if he occasionally buttoned him into a violet quilted bed jacket that had been his mother's (telling the nurse to humour a camp old man's little ways) it was done in a spirit of domestic spite not unlike that practised between many a cohabiting couple.

As a year went by, then two, during which his father was a powerless, dolled-up guest of honour at several of Perry's more Wildean parties, he came to think of the old man less as a parent than a grouchy partner. As he pecked his father's cheek on leaving for work or retiring for the night, as he amused himself by brushing his still thick, silver hair into a variety of fanciful styles, as he meticulously piped a saucily naked cherub onto his heart-shaped birthday cake, Perry would admit that, while still not exactly fond, he had developed a kind of tender dependence on his father's being there. Bereft of any other outlet, his nurturing energies were making do with the only available man on the horizon. (The nurse was never an option; Perry had old-fashioned views on the healthy inflexibility of sexual roles and had marked the nurse down as a sister from day one.)

Howard caught his eye over the contents of a dead woman's intestinal tract. The corpse had been principal stockholder in a toy manufacturing firm due for flotation. She was found face-down, fully dressed, in her sunken bath. Her family claimed she had drunk too much, fallen in, passed out and drowned. As detective inspector on the case,

Howard mistrusted them and ordered an autopsy. The stomach was duly shown to contain precious little bath water, which indicated that she had died before submersion. There was alcohol in her blood-stream but not enough to knock out, let alone kill, such a hardened drinker. Called in by the coroner to analyse the contents of her gut, Perry found beef, onions, red wine, button mushrooms, rice and significant traces of a powerful sedative administered to dogs and horses.

'Her brother's a vet,' Howard murmured. Beneath the crumpled, unshaven look of the overstressed detective, the ghost of a more dynamic person stirred. Leaning against the lab desk, he towered over Perry, who was perched on a stool. 'How specific can you be?'

'Very,' Perry told him, looking up from flicking through the pharmacology files on his computer screen. 'These weren't prescription tranqs. I mean, I can't give you a brand name but I can narrow it to a choice of six or seven and they're only for veterinary use.'

Now Howard smiled, a grin of broad satisfaction that cracked the laughter lines fanning out from his sad, blue eyes. Normally Perry was curt with policemen, judiciously telling them no more than the science they needed. Basking in the big man's approval, however, he would have prattled on for hours if it kept him so close.

'There's something else,' he added.

'What?'

'Well, it's much more concentrated in the gut contents samples than in her blood. Maybe it was injected into the meat they knew she was going to cook? If she ate it rare enough and they stuck enough in, it would still pack a lethal punch. You'll need to check my data with the coroner, but I think he'll bear it out.'

'Thanks,' Howard said. 'Thanks a lot. You've made my week. This could have turned messy.' He rubbed a big hand across his tired face and over his stubbled chin. 'I owe you a drink.'

'You're on.' Perry saw the wedding ring as he spoke.

From self-protective instinct he spent the rest of the day curbing his interest. When Howard dropped by late in the afternoon, however, changed, shaven and smelling of cheap cologne, he found it impossible to resist his invitation. Howard was a new transfer and unfamiliar with the area. On the pretext of showing him some countryside but actually to avoid running into any colleagues, Perry had him drive them out to a small country pub which served excellent pork and leek sausages. This proved a wise choice for, midway through his second pint, Howard lurched the conversation away from cadavers and poison to his marriage, his teenage daughter and, after much fumbling with a beer-mat, to the reason why his wife had left him. Perry discreetly rang the nurse and persuaded him to tuck his father up in bed and stay late on double time, then they drove up onto the moor and made frantic, bruising and extremely messy love in Howard's car.

Howard cried afterwards, which Perry found utterly bewitching.

They continued to meet regularly back in Howard's rented flat. Howard often cried out during sex or would exclaim, 'I like this. I *do*. This is what I like.' And he often wept after it for sheer relief. He claimed to find Perry overpowering because he could approach sex with another man so matter-of-factly. He had no idea that the very sight of him shyly unbuttoning his drip-dry shirt made Perry want to tap-dance. They always went to Howard's place. Perry found he could not face a meeting between his lover and his father, let alone Howard and the nurse and, when they first discussed their situations, had unthinkingly said that he 'lived with someone'. Howard's assumption that this was a lover and that Perry was risking a relationship to be with him gave Perry an even fizzier sense of power than Howard's grateful tears.

He said nothing to disabuse him. At first he liked the fact that their meetings were secret, snatched, and often in daylight. He liked the anonymity of Howard's drably furnished flat and the sense that it was an arena in which nothing was forbidden them. He soon began to grow hungry for more, however. He yearned for evenings together. He wanted to wake up with him. Most compellingly of all, he wanted to cook him a meal, the more so when he realized that Howard was a stranger to cookery and stocked nothing beyond teabags, cornflakes, butter, milk and a bag of sliced white.

Once he had settled upon fungi, of course, he had to wait a maddening four or five weeks until the most fitting ones were in season. He knew precisely the variety he needed to use. Mercifully rare, they happened to be a speciality of the region, favouring the grassy fringes of beech woods. Remarkably similar, at a glance, to an innocuous variety, the things had often been pointed out to him on walks with his mother. Identifiable only from the way their ghostly flesh bruised blue, they caused paralysis and, in an already weakened victim, heart failure. Taking care to use some kitchen towel to keep the toxic harvest separate from the harmless field mushrooms he had also picked, Perry made a perfect risotto; arborio rice brewed in chicken stock and mushroom juices – with a dash of cream and three threads of saffron – until sticky without being indigestibly glutinous. He went to some trouble. He lit candles and dressed his father in a jacket and tie.

'It could be our anniversary,' he told him as he spooned the fragrant mixture into the old man's eager mouth. 'More wine, dear? It's a good one this – nicely nutty without being sharp. There we go. Greedy! You'll have the end of the spoon off . . .'

He was not foolish. He waited, peacefully holding his father's hand as they listened to Mendelssohn, until it was plain that death had joined them at the table then he went to the telephone and summoned help. When he heard the ambulance approaching, he bravely wolfed down several mouthfuls of the bad risotto on top of the helping he had already eaten of the good. This meant that he was already feeling very cold and strange and barely needed to act when he begged the nice young man in casualty for a stomach pump.

'I don't know how I could have been so stupid,' he told his brothers later, his throat still raw. 'I've been picking mushrooms since we were children. I've never made a mistake before. I'll never forgive myself. Never.'

But he did, naturally. He bade the Irish nurse a tearful farewell, redecorated his father's room, donated two suitcases of old male clothes to Help the Aged and, at last, was in a position to invite Howard to dinner. He made the date for a Friday, intending them to spend the weekend together but had kept this last bit a surprise.

Howard brought flowers as well as wine. The leek tartlets were a triumph, as was the Moroccan chicken with salted lemons. Perry made a mental

39

note, however, never again to serve Howard lemon posset. He liked it almost too much and had a, somehow unromantic, second helping which brought on a nasty attack of heartburn come bedtime.

FOURTH OF JULY, 1862

Alice was beginning to get very tired of sitting by her sister on the bank, and of having nothing to do. Rhoda could sense her ennui just as she could feel the oppressive heat the child was giving off as she lolled heavily against her. Both were breaking her concentration on a peculiarly dry chapter she had just reached on the life cycle of the lobster.

Alice had yet to shake off the last of a heavy summer cold. She breathed through her mouth as she made a show of reading the book too. Rhoda could sense the desire to speak again welling up in the child. It was like the slow, fat bubble Papa used to amuse her with by upending then righting a tin of treacle.

Any minute now, Rhoda told herself.

Sure enough it was only moments later when Alice broke violently away in a bid to distract her further. 'A rabbit!' she shouted, pointing to the other side of the river. 'A white rabbit with pink eyes!'

Rhoda sighed and discreetly turned back a page to begin the chapter afresh. Heat and Alice had reduced it to mental fog. 'Don't be a tease, dear,' she murmured.

'But there was! It ran along the path there and dived through that long grass. It must have a hole there. And it had a waistcoat on and a pocket watch.'

'If only you'd brought your notebook you could have written me a story about it. I said I'd be dull company.'

'Yes, but somebody had to come with you,' said Alice with an unfortunate echo of their parlour maid, 'or people would talk.'

The family's maintenance of respectable behaviour was painfully erratic. Mama still thought nothing of sending Rhoda about town unchaperoned. She had allowed the question of whether Rhoda was *out* or not to slide in a way that left Rhoda known among her more orthodox peers as *Poor Rhoda* and which, she was quite sure, unsettled potential suitors. And, more importantly, their mothers. At Alice's age she had assumed she would one day have a coming-out dance then marry early and well. Young girls blithely assumed the inevitability of suitors as seeds did sunshine. Instead she found herself an old maid of eighteen with a mother more interested in moths than matrimony, doomed to become a governess if nobody would have her soon.

Her dreams of romantic escape to some more regular establishment had been easier to sustain while she was an only child but then she had been left at Miss Bileheart's academy while her parents made a two-year trip to Patagonia in search of some wasp or other and had returned with baby Alice tucked among their less lively specimens. The sisters had recently become fellows in suffering courtesy of a trip to Zanzibar that had produced Eustace. Rhoda felt more than ever the governess-to-be as Nanny was as taken up in the baby as Mama was in her lepidopterology, encouraging Alice to trail after her big sister for amusement.

In Rhoda's nightmares Alice was married off before her, a radiant child-bride in a foam of antique lace with Rhoda her embittered matron of honour in a dark violet silk with black trimmings and horrid jet beads.

'I'm bored,' Alice said, kicking out at a lizard and sending the poor innocent skittering into the long grass. 'Why couldn't we go to the museum to see the dodo?'

'We can't do that every Sunday, dear.'

'Or that garden? The pretty one with the fountains.'

'It's much cooler here,' Rhoda said although she agreed with her. She too loved the public gardens with their elegant benches, gravel walks and wealth of social opportunity. She had only chosen the secluded riverside walk instead in an effort to curb Alice's unseemly showing off by depriving her of a susceptible audience. 'If you keep very still, you might see a frog or a water vole.'

'I hate frogs.'

Rhoda sighed. *I sigh*, she thought, *more often than I laugh. No good can come of it. Soon I shall have a sighing sort of face and a downturned mouth.* 'Have another violet comfit,' she suggested.

Alice shook her head, her face like thunder. There were grass stains on her pinafore and gloves and one stocking was crumpled. She looked less than angelic. 'I'm thirsty,' she announced. A mother little older than herself staggered by under the weight of a large and especially piglike baby. Alice glared at the baby as though to blight it.

Rhoda reached guiltily into her reticule and took out a blue glass bottle. She had stolen it from the nursery cupboard that morning while Nanny was busy with Eustace's bath. She had taken to carrying a supply of her brother's gripe water the way women in the American West were said to carry pistols. It proved effective on her nerves in times of agitation and she hoped its soothing properties might still her sister. She could count on Alice's greed.

Alice snatched the bottle, unstoppered it and took a long, incautious draught before Rhoda could stop her. Then she flopped back on the rug beside her and closed her eyes. Rhoda retrieved what was left of the gripe water and returned to the life cycle of the lobster. But not for long.

'Which is that toadstool? You know, the one that gives you dreams?' Alice asked thoughtfully, eyes still closed.

'The Liberty Cap, psilocybe semilanceata. There were some in the field where we rested earlier.'

'If I ate it, would it make me sick?'

'Alice, you didn't!'

'No,' Alice said uncertainly. 'But if I did?'

'Possibly. You should certainly feel very strange.'

'Oh *good*!'

'But you're never to eat anything you find without showing me first.'

'I wish Dinah were with us.'

'You can't bring a cat on a picnic. It would be both eccentric and cruel. And you would most certainly lose the cat in the process.'

Alice snorted dismissively and shifted so that her head lay in Rhoda's lap. She yawned as might the cat in question, showing small white teeth and a curling tongue and fell asleep as abruptly as a kitten. Even allowing for her occasional snores, she looked, in slumber, as sweet as she appeared to be in company.

Until Alice took her first steps outside the nursery, Rhoda had thought herself fairly attractive, not unchastely witty, an attentive listener, in short, a girl any man might wish to marry. But even before Alice could lisp complete sentences, she had eclipsed her. She was unambiguously beautiful, petulant and given to wild fancies. Men of all ages, Papa included, found her delightful. Were Mama less vague about observing proprieties it would not have mattered but Alice rarely stayed in a room when sent to it and encroached on Rhoda's shrinking territory at all hours. She had only to appear, clutching the dormouse she kept in a straw-lined teapot or begging to recite *'Tis the Voice of the Sluggard* or *Speak Gently, It Is Better Far* for Rhoda to feel herself dull, humourless and overlooked. She lacked charm, she had discovered, and resented those who had failed to instil it in her, which only emphasized the shortcoming.

As if to illustrate the problem, The Mathematician now came by in his rowing boat. Rhoda just had time to slide Alice's hot little head off her lap and onto a cushion before he came ashore.

Two years ago he would not have been her first choice. With his stoop and whiskers he seemed almost as old as Papa and it was hard to picture him as an object of devotion but he remained the most prominent bachelor among her parents' friends and the most regular caller at their house.

'Chaperone asleep on the job?' he asked after they had exchanged hellos.

'Yes and *please* don't wake her. She's been a trial because I dared to thwart her.'

They sat together a little further off in a willow's shifting shade. The air was thick with river scents and the cooing of wood pigeons. Warm from his rowing and apologetically in shirtsleeves, he was far more appealing and youthful than she had ever known him. He smelled of laundry starch and something more manly.

She fed him tarts from the picnic hamper, confessing she had made the mulberry jam herself but not the pastry and, for the first time in their acquaintance, she felt he was noticing her.

'Do you dance?' he asked her and she felt herself blush absurdly as she replied that of course she did.

'When required to,' she added then wished she hadn't because it made it sound as though she danced only under sufferance when, on the contrary, it was one of her chiefest pleasures, second only to reading.

'So do you know a dance called the Lancers' Quadrille?' he asked.

'I love it,' she told him, to correct her earlier cold impression.

'How many pairs does one need to perform it successfully, I wonder?'

Was he planning a dance? The idea was strange, almost comical, but not impossible. He could not give it in his college, of course, but it was not unheard of for bachelor dons to entertain in the assembly rooms or under the aegis of married friends. For a wild moment she imagined him

49

waltzing her through her father's library, her skirts raising a small tornado of disturbed papers and index cards about them.

'It's for a poem,' he explained, abashed. 'However fanciful the destination, I like to embark from a rock of sound fact.'

Discovering he was a poet transformed him almost as much as finding him in shirtsleeves had done.

She answered his strange question and decided she would beg Mama to throw a dance for her, however modest, and see that he was invited. She allowed him to look with curiosity at the book she was reading. Talk of lobsters led to talk of lunch, because he had been served mock turtle soup that day and it seemed she genuinely fascinated him by being able to explain that marine turtles only appeared to be weeping when out of the water because their kidneys could not break down brine so it was constantly discharged from a gland like a tear duct beside each eye.

A puppy loitering behind its walkers threatened to wake Alice by licking her face and hands. Worried she was coming across as too drily academical, Rhoda seized the chance to reveal her tender potential by shooing the puppy off and sliding Alice's head back onto her lap. Alice mumbled crossly but slept on and Rhoda spread her golden hair across her skirt so that some of Alice's loveliness might reflect up on her.

Of course his eye was now repeatedly drawn to the wretched child and he began to talk so warmly about the poignant brevity of youthful innocence that Rhoda was tempted to rouse her sister at once, Alice having a reliably filthy temper when woken abruptly. Instead she grew cool and formal and must have repelled him because he soon apologized for keeping her from her studies. Despite a rather unseemly, even desperate, late offer of another jam tart, he took his leave and rowed away.

She abandoned her reading and ate the last tart herself. Then, in a sudden access of spite, she roused Alice by shaking leaves into her face from an overhanging branch. Alice woke in such a state of excitement and so full of some vivid dream she had been enjoying that Rhoda feared she had been nibbling hallucinogenic fungus after all.

As Alice finally wandered off and began to amuse herself, Rhoda felt a chill breeze across her heart and suffered an insidious fancy that her life was no more than an unimportant fiction and that any instant an impatient hand would turn the page and she and her crossness and her compendium of facts and her lack of charm would be gone.

She resolved to be a sweeter sister, at least for what remained of the summer.

SAVING SPACE

'Is this place taken?'

'No. Not at all.'

Although the church porch was quite empty, he instinctively rose slightly and slid along on the stone bench to make room for her. Shyness had become a philosophy with him. Throughout their marriage, his wife had always talked to strangers for him, filling the air with words enough for two. Since her death he had developed tactics for evading conversation. On a train or aeroplane or in a dentist's waiting room, he would read or summon up an appearance of such profound concentration as to offer a mute rebuke to any who might think to interrupt his chain of thought. Formalized exchanges with waiters or ticket sellers were easily got through but he had learned to dread the formless conversation of strangers; one never knew where it might lead.

Settling back on the bench, he faced slightly away from her, towards the closed church door. He had not thought to bring a book and clutched only a cushion. His wife had always said that part of the fun of concerts at Trenellion was the lack of seat reservations. Places had to be reserved with cushions, an hour before each festival concert began. This task had always fallen to his wife, who relished the conversations she initiated while queuing and would season each interval in the concert with pinches of information she had gleaned.

'That one there. In the purple. On her second marriage. He's a bone-cracker from St Tudy.'

'See that one? No. Over there by the organ bench. With the funny teeth? Three children in the orchestra this year. Just imagine. Three! Wife not musical at all, apparently. Odd how that happens sometimes. Like vicars with wives who don't do flowers.'

This was his first time back since her death. For four summers in a row he had preferred to let the cottage throughout the season and stay put in Barrowcester, weathering the heat and the tourists. This year, however, his teenage granddaughters had expressed a wish to learn to surf. He had been perfectly willing to let his son and his family have the place to themselves but had been hectored into coming too. His daughter-in-law, who worked as a bereavement counsellor in her spare time, accused him of avoiding memories.

'They're happy memories,' he said. 'Why should I want to avoid them?'

So he had come, clinging at least to the independence his own car afforded, and found his quiet, seaside cottage turned into a kind of purgatory. The bathroom was rarely free when he needed it, the radio had always been tuned away from Radio 3 when he turned it back on, his son kept cornering him with grotesque expressions of hangdog sympathy, his daughter-in-law had a way of ruining perfectly good food by cooking it with fashionable herbs that all smelt more or less of tomcat, and his granddaughters, tall, tanned, muscular creatures like athletes from a Nazi propaganda film, only with less manners, persisted in holding open house to all manner of nouveau-louche youth they attracted on the beach.

The festival's fortnight of nightly concerts was proving his salvation. Playing on the family's aversion to classical music, he bought a fistful of single tickets, cheap at the price, and escaped every afternoon at five-thirty to wait at the front of the queue. He then enjoyed a reassuringly plain, unvarying picnic of boiled eggs, pork pies, tomatoes and red wine before the concert and returned home after it able to face his son's patronage and granddaughters' partying with a measure of equanimity. There were just three concerts to go, three more nights of sanity after which he would make good his escape.

'Excuse me.'

She was a young-old girl, hair in slides, in an ill-fitting floral frock. From its dusty quality and fifties style, it might have come from one of the charity shops he gathered the young now frequented.

'Yes?'

'I know it's an awful cheek but would you mind taking this and bagging a seat for me?' She held out a cushion as faded as her dress, saw his hesitation. 'It's just that I so want a good seat but I ought to be helping in the car park.'

'Oh. Yes. Of course.' He took the cushion and was charmed by her smile. Music student, he thought. Nice, old-fashioned kind of girl. The sort who would play the viola from choice.

He saved her a seat across the aisle from him, so she would not feel bound to make grateful conversation later on. He looked out for her as he ate his solitary picnic but the only car park attendants he saw were girls like his granddaughters, in shorts, sharing a bottle of wine and making fun of drivers who disliked reversing. Perhaps she had chosen to guard the lay-by, a solitary job.

He grew mildly anxious as the church filled and still she failed to appear. When a festival official came to stare at the offending, sought-after space and he explained it was for a car parker, the cushion was briskly whisked away.

'She can stand at the back like the rest of us,' the official said and gave the seat to a tall man with a cough.

Worried, he looked for her in the interval after the first piece, a jubilant Bach motet, but the people standing at the back were unfamiliar. Then he reflected that her face was so quiet he would probably look straight through her if he saw her again. He gave himself over to the pleasures of music and thought nothing more of it.

That night he could not sleep. His room felt airless and seemed haunted by a sweet smell whose source he could not place.

The next concert was chamber music – two string quartets and an obscure Swiss piece involving trombones. The crowd would not be large, therefore, but chamber concerts tended to involve extra competition for a pew with a view, so he came early and once again found himself one of the few people in the porch. He remembered to bring a book as defence, a guide to seventeenth-century bench ends.

'Excuse me?'

A middle-aged woman with a defeated air, she had on a oatmeal-coloured trouser suit of the kind he recalled his wife wearing under Heath. He was irritated at the interruption but no sooner met her eye than he felt oddly protective towards her.

'Yes?'

'I wonder if I could rely on you to save a space for me with this.'

He felt one of the momentary qualms that had become so frequent since he became a widower; did he know her? He had never been good at remembering people, especially women. This was partly his wife's fault, of course, because she remembered absolutely everyone and, like an ambassador's private secretary, would second-guess when he was at a loss and would discreetly murmur a name in his ear as an unfamiliar face approached. Matters weren't helped by the way Trenellion drew on such a shallow pool socially that concerts were full of men and women of a similar age and type. The women tended to be nicely weather-beaten, gardening, dogwalking sorts with unfussy, undyed hair, many of whom looked remarkably alike to his eyes.

'It's my mother, you see,' the woman continued. 'I can't leave her for long. I mean I can, obviously, for the concert, but the friend who's mummy-sitting won't arrive until half-past.'

'Of course,' he told her and smiled in case he did know her. 'I'll do my best.'

He saw the way other people in the queue glared at him as he took the old cushion off her. *Queuebargers*, they were thinking, *quislings,* but their glares hardened his resolve. His wife's mother passed her last eight years in their spare room. He knew what it cost to ask for help.

Sure enough, the audience was not large, but the seat he had saved her beside him was put at threat by a lively clutch of people who expressed a wish to sit by their friends.

'Tell you what,' said their ringleader. 'We'll sit and chat till she gets here and then when she comes we can all bunch up.'

He was on the point of saying that the pews only sat four in any comfort when he thought he recognized one of the group as a schoolfriend of his son. Inhibited, he fell to reading programme notes and let them annex the pew. The later the woman was, the wilder his pledges to himself, until he reached the point of being prepared to give up his seat for her. She never returned, however, and her cushion went from being merely squeezed to being sat upon by a stranger. Perhaps the mother had taken a turn for the worse, he thought.

The trombone piece proved surprisingly beguiling.

Driving home, dazzled by headlamps in his rear-view mirror, he could not rid himself of the sense that he was not alone in the car. Even with the window wide, the sweet smell in his room was more powerful than ever. Ridiculously unnerved, he stayed up to party with the granddaughters and their ghastly friends and woke in an armchair in the small hours with a crick in his neck and a strange dog on his lap that showed its teeth when he made to move.

The final concert of the season, a Mozart triple bill, drew a huge crowd, far more than could fit in the church. Many would content themselves with lolling against tombstones near the open doors. Even leaving the cottage at five-thirty he found the end of the queue outside the porch already. He drew up a plastic chair like the others but kept himself aloof from the prevailing Dunkirk spirit with the aid of J.T. Blight's *Churches of West Cornwall*.

'Excuse me.'

One could see at a glance she was frail, with legs like matchsticks and a shakiness to the hand that grasped the cushion. She began to explain that she had promised to collect a friend but he cut her short, taking the cushion from her with a smile, won over by a nostalgic waft of Yardley's English Lavender.

He moved with low cunning and secured two of the best seats in the house. He took the precaution of cutting his picnic short, stinting on the red wine so as to be back at their cushions in good time. He defended her place from all comers. When, at the eleventh hour, the chorus and orchestra already in place, an imperious woman in black satin said, 'I really must ask you to give up that seat. Seven-thirty is the absolute cut-off point for reservations and we still have a queue,' his reaction took him by surprise.

62

'It's my wife,' he told her. 'She is coming, she's desperate to, but she's very ill you see and can't queue for long. She'll be here any second, I'm certain of it.'

To his amazement the woman melted and was almost placatory. 'Of *course* she will,' she said. 'That's quite all right.'

He realized to his horror that she had been a friend, if not quite an intimate, of his late wife and plainly thought he had lost his reason to grief. Shamefaced, he turned swiftly to face the front again, praying no one else had overheard his words who knew the truth of the matter and might report the story back to his son.

As the conductor swept through the applause to his podium and still the old woman had not appeared, he noticed her cushion for the first time. It was a sun-bleached affair in dog-worn chintz. An honourable, holiday cottage sort of cushion, that spoke of long afternoons and sweet, familiar pleasures. The same cushion he had taken from strange, female hands the night before and the night before that.

Instinctively he withdrew his hand from it and sat to one side, giving it space.

'As some of you may realize,' the conductor was saying, 'tonight's performance is dedicated to Betty Pearson, who cheerfully dubbed herself *spinster of this parish* and was for four decades a crucial, modest, background figure in keeping the festival ticking over. She died last week. Dear Betty, we know you're listening. This one's for you.'

As the overture to *Così* bubbled around them, he became aware of the smell again, the sweet smell that had twice invaded his bedroom. He heard the unmistakable rustle of cellophane and the muffled clunk of happily sucked boiled sweet bumping tooth. No one else seemed to be bothered by it and before long the music had cleared all other thoughts and sensations from his head. Hours later, however, rinsing out his picnic things, he was so startled that he stumbled back and sat on the kitchen stool, tap still running.

In the small Tupperware box where he had left no more than an uneaten tomato and some salt in a small twist of foil, someone had tucked an unopened bag of barley sugars.

PETALS ON A POOL

Edith was only at the festival because of an administrative error. It was the *other* Edith Chalmers they'd wanted. She knew it, her agent knew it and so – rapidly – did the festival organizers but two decades of such slights at last gave rise to a small demonstration of bloody-mindedness and she affected not to have understood, which duly shamed everyone else into saying nothing.

She was the first Edith Chalmers. She wrote quietly devastating studies of a quiet sort of English character: thwarted people too well bred to fight, people who numbered priests among their friends, people who not only noticed split infinitives but found them morally troubling. The other Edith Chalmers, who had no such qualms, wrote bestsellers about illegitimate girls of no account who rose to positions of tediously itemized wealth and high status. She only bothered to call herself Edith P. Chalmers for her first offering, *To Boldly Sin*. The sales of this eclipsed all those of her namesake in less than two weeks and the P. was dropped from the second edition. It was the kind of effrontery that she celebrated in her heroines.

The first Edith naïvely thought her publishers might sue but they merely resorted to a suitably quiet sort of branding, thereafter announcing her as Edith Chalmers (Author of *Sad Cypresses*) or Edith Chalmers (Author of *A Corner Table*).

'You've been invited to the Bali Book Festival,' her agent said warily. 'All expenses paid. They want you for a spotlight session and then a panel on romantic fiction. Shall I let them down gently?'

Edith would usually have sighed and said yes but she thought of her late best friend Margaret, who had written whodunits about a dog breeder and said yes to everything. Margaret was a tireless attendee of readers' days and book festivals and regarded each and every train ticket, hotel bed and feast of mini-bar chocolate as just compensation for the failure of her publishers to see that her lengthy backlist took fire. Margaret remained a shameless freeloader until her recent death. Edith missed her keenly.

'No,' she told her agent. 'Say yes for a change. Tell them I'd be delighted.'

She assumed the organizers would find a way to

cancel once they'd seen their mistake but perhaps, being oriental, they were too strenuously polite. They e-mailed gushingly to say how wonderful, what fans they were and so on. Then they e-mailed again, rather more coolly, to say how unexpectedly difficult they were finding it to gather sufficient stock of her titles for the festival bookshop. They sent her aeroplane ticket with nothing more enthusi-astic attached than a compliment slip. It was only an economy ticket – the other Edith lived in a tax haven and passed much of her life in first class – but this Edith was slight and would be perfectly comfortable. It would be a free holiday with only a little work attached, it would be interesting and it would offer some correction to the disparity in her and her namesake's fortunes.

As she fought through the airport crowds into the stifling evening air of Denpasar, Edith faced humiliation by taxi driver. Ranged along a crowd barrier was a three-deep line of drivers, all holding cards with the names of the passengers they were there to collect. She could see her name nowhere but some of the writing was small. She unearthed her glasses then walked along the line squinting at the names, a process made no easier by the way each driver waggled his card as she drew close, blur-ring its lettering. She walked up and down four times, melting in the heat, bitterly regretting her decision to come, and was at last reduced to perching on her sagging suitcase, in full view of all the drivers, to wait.

Her name appeared at last, wildly misspelt, behind all the others, waggled by a driver who explained, entirely without apology, that they had still to wait for someone else.

'Might I sit in the car at least?' she asked but he only smiled and repeated,

'We have to wait, lady. Very important guest.'

This proved to be a formidable journalist from Hong Kong, Lucinda Yeung. Lent height by heels, soignée to the point of agelessness, she made Edith conscious of the crumpled hours she had just passed in travelling. She had a set of immaculate suitcases, of a shade that toned with her cream suit, and left their driver to cope with them while she consulted her little kid-bound agenda and quizzed Edith. As soon as she'd ascertained that she wasn't the other Edith Chalmers, she relaxed and confessed to having 'stitched her up once'. She broke off to grill the driver in quickfire Bahasa then turned back with a feline smile. 'Turns out we're staying in the island's best hotel,' she said. 'You're very lucky. The drive will take around thirty-five minutes. Do you mind if I conduct a little business? I'm chairing several events and I'm way behind as always.'

Edith said that would be quite understandable and Ms Yeung spent the rest of their blissfully air-conditioned journey on her telephone, greeting a succession of authors with virtually identical praise for their latest books and the bluntly delivered instruction that they were not to turn up for their events with prepared speeches.

'The public comes to see you interact, not reading your homework. And they don't want readings either; they can read your book themselves once you've convinced them to buy it.'

The end of each call was softened by some variant of the praise that had opened it and some regally personal touch, an enquiry about a garden or husband or pet made after a rapid glance at the notes she had made alongside the names and addresses in her agenda. A call completed, a name was scratched off a list. Ms Yeung's professionalism was so astonishing it did not occur to Edith to be offended or to make any effort not to listen in.

The last author was dealt with as they finished passing through Ubud, roughly five minutes before their arrival at the hotel. Ms Yeung put away her agenda and gave Edith her full, interested attention.

'Don't worry that we're so far out from all the action,' she told her. 'There'll be a free car to take you into Ubud whenever you need and the compensations are terrific. The nights are cooler and quieter out here. You won't be troubled by barking dogs or woken by cockerels and the rooms and service are perfection.'

The car paused at a gatehouse for security men to check beneath it for bombs then they were waved through. They approached a brightly-lit pavilion, where staff were lined up in expectation.

'Now don't go racing off with your famous friends tomorrow. I'll want to catch up with you,' Ms Yeung said as a young man in a version of traditional dress came to open their door.

Female staff met them with namastes and draped them with scented white garlands of welcome. Then, before Edith could say goodnight, they were deftly separated and whisked in different directions into the lantern-lit grounds.

It was like no hotel she had ever visited. There was none of the usual sordid business of credit-card swipes or checking who was paying for what. Edith's guide introduced herself as Ayu.

'I'm your personal assistant for the duration of your stay. Anything you need, anything you don't like, just dial one and I'll answer,' she said. 'I'll stop by each morning after breakfast to file your requests for the day. Your room is this way. Watch your step here, it's a little uneven.'

She led the way past a bewildering succession of pavilions and pools, gardens and terraces. She pointed out various restaurants and spa centres in passing which Edith was sure she would never rediscover by daylight. Edith could hear rushing water somewhere far below and, through the trees, a music like nothing she had heard before, at once frenetic and calmly circular, as though moving at two speeds at once. It seemed to be made by gongs or tuned drums of some kind.

'It's a temple ceremony,' Ayu told her, seeing she had paused to listen. 'There's a full moon this week . . . So. Here we are. This is your room and your own pool is just there across the terrace. Beyond that grille you'll find a library with a computer and broadband access.'

She unlocked and slid open a huge glazed door into a suite of rooms easily the size of Edith's little flat in Tufnell Park. She demonstrated shower, fridge, television, lighting, remote control, air con-ditioning, mosquito nets and only then, on the point of bidding goodnight and as though she sensed it was deeply distasteful, she asked for Edith's pass-port and took a swipe of her credit card on a tiny electronic reader she produced from a pocket.

After a dreamy night haunted by the sound of distant gongs and the perfume of aromatic oil in the lanterns on her terrace, Edith woke to find herself in a kind of paradise. The hotel was a series of taste-fully converted antique buildings spread across an old estate or plantation on the steeply folded sides of a river valley. Through the trees came virid glimpses of deserted rice fields but no other buildings.

Edith had been trained by Margaret never to have a hotel breakfast delivered for fear of extra charges and a reduction in choice. Besides, breakfast in a pretty pavilion built over a cascade was part of the treat. Deciding not to fret after English marmalade and her usual toast and strong coffee, she elected to embrace, with a good child's passivity, whatever this adventure threw at her. She thus found herself sipping a lawn-green concoction made of melon and parsley and eating some kind of pancakes stuffed with nuts and berries.

It was impossible to sense how many guests there were since they were housed far apart and many, like Ms Yeung, might have elected to take breakfast on their terraces. The restaurant was almost deserted. There was a severe Japanese woman glaring into her tea in a corner and an Australian couple were leaving, softly arguing, as she arrived. At the table next to her a wan young man was poring over the festival programme. He smiled fleetingly and mouthed a hello at her as she sat so it didn't seem too forward to speak back once she had finished the last of her surprisingly filling pancakes.

'Are you here for the festival too?'

'Looks like it,' he said quietly.

'Are you Irish?'

'American,' he said. 'But my mother was from Limerick.' He looked back at the programme. 'My event seems to have been left off this.'

'How terrible! Is it too late to complain?'

'Oh I'm used to it. A voice in the wilderness, that's me.'

'I'm Edith Chalmers,' she said brightly, in an effort to head him off from gloom.

He brightened at once. 'No!'

'The other one. The one no one's heard of.'

'Ah. Well no one's heard of me either so we're quits. I'm Peter John.' He leant across to shake her proffered hand. His grasp was so cool and weak she wondered if he were unwell. 'You see? You've forgotten it already. I always told my mother it was a mistake to marry a man with no proper surname; two first names give the mind no anchor.'

'I'll think of you as Prester John,' she said. 'Then it'll stick. Sorry. What do you write?'

'I'm a poet,' he said. 'So my case is hopeless really. Still, we're in the very best hotel and I intend to make the most of it. Although even the staff seem to have forgotten I'm here.'

As if on cue, the waitress ignored his pleading look as she came to clear Edith's place. Edith offered him a roll and nut butter as he looked famished but he waved her little basket aside.

'No thanks,' he said. 'I've a massage at ten and it's best on an empty stomach. They're going to pound me with sea salt then dribble me all over with stimulating oils. But show me your event so I can circle it.'

She flicked through his programme and shyly pointed out her two events, feeling she ought really to give him one of them. He circled them both with a tiny pen worthy of Ms Yeung. It was ivory with a little skull carved on its cap.

'If I hear no one else,' he said, 'I shall come into town to hear you, the other, the *real* Edith Chalmers!'

Although her events were not until the third day, she felt honour bound to attend as much of the festival as possible because someone else had paid for her to be there and she had been nicely brought up. Besides, the hotel's luxury – a part of which plainly lay in its keeping the vulgar question of prices aired as rarely as possible – made her nervous. It might have been different had someone from the festival welcomed her and made it quite clear what she was and wasn't going to be paying for at the adventure's end . . .

So for two days she fought jet-lag and lived like a nun among sybarites, eating minimal breakfasts, catching her free ride into Ubud in the morning and dining in the evening off the treats in her lavishly restocked fruit bowl, which Ayu had expressly pointed out were free of charge. By day she heard novelists and translators and historians and poets. She sat through discussions of adultery in young adult fiction, the gender politics of far eastern folklore and Does Post Colonialism Exist. She winced at one woman's account of her daughter's circumcision and laughed at another's sonnet to her neurotic Abyssinian. It was all very lively and interesting but she felt lonely in a way she never felt at home, where she saw far fewer people. She longed to escape and explore the island, which clearly had a unique and fascinating culture, but she was intimidated by her lack of language and the vast denominations of the local currency. She felt she shouldn't go touring during festival hours yet when the last event finished it was nearly dark and she was nervous of missing her free ride home.

She spotted Lucinda Yeung repeatedly, either on stage or in the middle of an animated crowd, but Ms Yeung's glance seemed to slide over her in a myopic way that discouraged friendly approaches. The other writers all seemed to know each other and wandered off to socialize in merry groups but nobody thought to ask Edith along, perhaps because she had removed her author's badge when she tired of explaining why she couldn't sign the other Edith Chalmers' books.

Massage, she was startled to gather, seemed to be playing a greater part in the festival for most writers than literature. Whenever she listened in on an offstage conversation, writers seemed to be comparing notes on which kind of pummelling, stretching or kneading had worked best for them so far, which day spa offered the best value and which the most handsome or beautiful practitioners.

Her lifeline, on the second day, was Peter John. He seemed to have been as overlooked as she was. Not only was he not in the programme but no badge had been made up for him and the shop had stocked none of his books. He seemed quite unabashed. He fashioned his own author badge which read *Peter John: Neglected Poet*!

Whenever he saw her he came to sit by her to gossip for a while or simply make her feel less unattached in the crowds. Madame Yeung, he assured her, was far too grand to chat to either of them now that her column was so widely syndicated around the Pacific rim and her cable show had taken off. 'Consider yourself honoured she gave you five minutes in the taxi from the airport,' he said. 'She stood up Seamus Heaney and they say she once made Peggy Atwood cry, which must take some doing.'

Undaunted at being left off the programme, he made regular use of the open mike sessions during the lunch hour, reciting his poetry by heart to the near-empty auditorium in his whispery voice until jostled off the stage by someone else who acted as though he wasn't there. Edith was not a poetry-reader by habit but she liked his. His verses were dry and witty and desperately sad and she couldn't think why he wasn't famous, especially as he was so pale and interesting.

'I don't care,' he assured her, as though reading her mind. 'Really I don't. I'm here. That's what matters. And my poems are all out there. Somewhere.' He glared towards the bookshop. 'Frankly I'm really more interested in the pursuit of deep relaxation. I'm running up a vast bill on massages at the hotel. Heaven knows how I'll pay for it. I suppose I'll just have to watch my card go into meltdown. The deep tissue man is a genius. And there's a Javanese woman, unexpectedly stout, who does incredible things with jets of warm water. You should try it, Edith. Give yourself a lift before your big day.'

But she doubted him. She watched him when he didn't know she was watching, scanning the poetry shelves to look at the fat, signed piles of his rivals' work or reciting his poems while three Australian women loudly disagreed with one another about Sufism, oblivious to him. She believed he was slighted at every turn. When they caught the car back to the hotel, she had to stop the driver from leaving without giving him time to climb aboard. And, for all his talk of the wonderful massages he was getting, the hotel staff seemed to pay him as little heed as they did the geckos which chuckled so startlingly from the restaurant eaves.

She felt their interest in her slacken too, once Ayu realized she wasn't going to book a chakra realignment or a colonic irrigation. Ayu was still there to greet her each morning as she emerged for breakfast, but by the third day she did so with a singsong slackness that hinted at mockery.

Edith's events were both, in their way, disasters. Her spotlight session had a tiny, restless audience because she was programmed, in the smallest auditorium, at the same time as the latest Indian prize-winner was packing out the big one. As for her panel discussion on romantic fiction, her attempt to take the subject seriously, although she was by no means a romantic novelist, went for naught because one of her fellow panellists had broken the agreement and written a lengthily tedious speech, not remotely on the topic, which she insisted she had to read as she had been up half the night writing it. After which there were only fifteen minutes left for their moderator – not alas the implacable Ms Yeung – to ask the rest of them one question each.

But Peter came to both sessions and so, astonishingly, did Lucinda Yeung, although she did not sit rapt as he did but took such repeated notes in her agenda that Edith suspected she was merely claiming the nearest convenient chair while she prepared for her next session with someone more newsworthy.

'I feel I've seen nothing of Bali,' Edith confided in Peter, once she had explained to the only audience member to ask that no, the bookshop had only managed to stock one of her earliest books, not the latest and that all the others were by a quite different Edith Chalmers. 'And it's my last night. It seemed criminal doing nothing but coming to festival events and walking in the hotel grounds.'

He convinced her to stay on in Ubud as night fell and the streets began to buzz with scooters. 'But I've left all my cash at the hotel so you'll have to be Sugar Mother,' he said with an unexpected wink.

That was fine by her. When she last counted her

rupiahs on her bed she seemed to have over a million still.

He said he wasn't hungry since that morning's particularly strenuous massage seemed to have wiped out his appetite, but he encouraged her to take a table in the Café Lotus to drink a delicious cocktail of lemongrass, lime juice and pressed ginger then he led her off down some lively side streets to a little restaurant, where they seemed to be the only big-boned Westerners, and chose for her a sequence of small dishes of fish and chicken that seemed the very essence of exotic travel after her lonely plunderings of her fruit bowl.

Finally he led her to a neighbourhood temple. A full moon ceremony was building up to some kind of climax or at least was in full flow. The steps were busy with worshippers coming and going, the air bright with the jangling melodies of the percussion orchestra he explained was called a gamelan. It would have felt quite wrong to go inside as they weren't Hindus but he found a comfortably low wall outside where they sat for a happy hour smelling incense and frangipani, listening to the music and hubbub and marvelling at the elegance with which local women could ride side-saddle on their husbands' scooters while balancing little towers of fruit or rice cakes on their heads to offer at the altars within.

'I think this is why I became a writer,' she found

herself saying suddenly. 'For the excuse it gives simply to sit quietly and watch.' And, sitting and watching, she spotted several writers from the festival walking by and she felt gratifyingly less of a tourist than they were, simply by virtue of sitting still. 'Thank you,' she said at last. 'Thank you for that.' Lent courage by having a pale and interesting young poet at her side, she had no trouble in hailing them a taxi back to the hotel.

They rode in silence but there was no awkwardness because the driver's radio was serenading them with flute music. When she caught Peter's eye occasionally, as they bumped around a corner or swerved to avoid a precariously laden scooter, he smiled at her before looking back at the passing night scenes.

'Can you really not pay your bill?' she asked at last as they were walking back through the grounds.

'Oh. Probably not. But it couldn't matter less. I'll plead ignorance, say I thought it was all covered by the festival. It couldn't matter less, honestly, Edith. I have been here before.'

She realized they had observed none of the usual literary festival etiquette of exchanging addresses or cards or assurances to review one another favourably but he had cast a kind of spell on the evening's end so they merely shook hands and he melted peaceably into the scented night. The scent, she had discovered by now, was nothing more exotic than citronella oil burning in the little lanterns on every surface to discourage mosquitoes, but she was still enchanted by it and by the elegance with which the lanterns had been used instead of banal electric light to outline flights of steps around the grounds.

She packed everything but the clothes she would be travelling in and the unwieldy Norwegian novel she had yet to finish. Then she sat out on her terrace, feasting shamelessly on fruit she couldn't name and listening to the gentle plashing of water in her infinity pool and the distant flutes and drums coming from a temple that had been silent every night until now.

What, she wondered, would her friend Margaret have done differently had she been there? Struck up useful friendships, certainly. Left with invitations to festivals in Kuala Lumpur and Shanghai all but confirmed. Eaten more. Drunk more. But Edith doubted she would have befriended Peter John. At heart, like most crime writers, Margaret was a social conservative and his pale and interesting qualities, his lack of vim, would have repelled her.

Edith ate the last rambutan in the bowl, dabbed her chin with a napkin and decided that when she got home she would institute some changes. She might even do what her agent had been suggesting for years and write something wildly different under a pseudonym. Something with sex and risk. Something with a plot.

She woke very early, as she always did the night before a long journey. Once she'd dressed and thrown back the curtains, she saw Ayu had not yet taken up her usual patient position on one of the terrace chairs. But perhaps that was because it was her last day and there could be no question of her suddenly requiring excursions or treatments.

Despite the terrific heat, she had not once swum in her pool because it had not occurred to her to bring a swimming costume to a book festival. She appreciated the pool as a thing of beauty, though, lined with slate tiles and reflecting the canopy of great trees overhead. The wind must have risen a little overnight for each morning the pool's surface had been thinly carpeted with leaves which a groundsman would patiently extract with a rake while she was at breakfast.

This morning there were petals as well as leaves, as though some crimson shrub had shed all its blossom in the night. And, inches beneath them, Peter John was floating, open eyes to the morning sky, dressed in his habitual linen trousers and baggy white shirt. He looked paler than ever, as though the moonlit water had chilled him from merely pale to a silvery kind of blue.

She knelt at once and, dropping her book and spectacle case, tried to grasp his trailing shirt tails. He was floating just beyond her reach however and she was fearful of falling in herself. Growing breathless, she stood, glancing about her, and called out, 'Hello?' Her voice sounded especially feeble and bloodlessly English against the exotic birdsong and rustling of leaves. Usually the grounds were discreetly busy with staff by this hour. There always seemed to be a gardener raking up fallen leaves or one of the smarter-dressed personal assistants ferrying a guest in a buggy, but for once there was nobody in view. Edith hurried back inside, fumbling to fit her key into the lock with shaking fingers, and dialled 1.

'There's a man in my pool, Ayu. A fellow guest. I . . . I think he's drowned,' she said.

The sofa was immensely deep and comfortable and she found she had no power to leave it now she had sat. Perhaps she had not slept as well as she'd thought. Feeling her sixty-nine years, sweating despite the air conditioning, she waited and ate a grape or two abstractedly. Then she heard voices by the pool: a man's and a woman's, Ayu's. Ayu sounded almost angry but then she appeared at Edith's door, utterly composed, and tapped lightly on the glass.

'Miss Chalmers? Are you all right?'

'Yes. I'm fine,' Edith said, forcing herself to rise. 'It was a bit of a shock, that's all.'

'Er. There is no one in the pool, Miss Chalmers. Here. Come and see.'

One of the groundsmen, his skin far darker than Ayu's, was raking the leaves and petals off the water and heaping them in a shallow, woven basket.

Peter was no longer there. The groundsman saw her staring and said something in Bahasa. Ayu snapped back at him but he smiled at Edith and she felt stupid.

'I'm so sorry to have alarmed you all,' she said.

'That's all right. There were a lot of flowers on the water. Perhaps it was a trick of the light?'

'Yes. Of course. Yes. I'm sure that's all it was. I'm so very sorry.'

'I've had them bring your breakfast to the terrace,' Ayu added. 'In case you were . . .' She sought the correct word and, as always, her cautious use of an idiom highlit its strangeness. 'In case you were *not quite yourself*.'

'How kind.'

'Your flight for Singapore leaves at twelve forty-five so I'll bring the buggy for you at a quarter to ten.'

'Thank you. And will you bring my bill then?'

'Your bill? Oh. Please, Miss Chalmers, there is nothing for you to pay.'

'Nothing? But I had several breakfasts. And snacks.'

'Nothing. Enjoy your breakfast.'

Ayu performed a tidy namaste and withdrew via the poolside where she dropped her courteous tone to deliver another clattering rebuke to the groundsman.

There were several altars about the place, lapped

in the black and white checked cloth Peter had explained symbolized the perfectly maintained balance of good and evil. Every morning someone left fresh offerings on them, Lilliputian arrangements of flowers and fruit on a leaf, usually with a smouldering incense stick in their midst. One saw these everywhere in Ubud, not just on altars but on the pavements and thresholds, protecting a house from unhappy spirits presumably. Edith had assumed that the hotel altars were purely decorative, like the faux-antique Buddhist or Hindu statues she had seen tourists showing off to one another at the festival. But perhaps not? Perhaps they were ancient sites of worship that long predated this artificial, impeccably staffed Eden.

As Edith obediently sipped her Juice of the Day – carrot, papaya and lime, a little card informed her – she saw an old woman, surely too roughly dressed to be a member of staff, placing a fresh offering at the altar that lay between her terrace and the point where the hotel grounds gave way to the dazzling green of the rice fields.

Edith forced herself to eat her pancakes, as they were probably the last wholesome food that would be set before her for twenty-four hours. She watched the old woman finish her interesting combination of prayers and housekeeping at the altar and make her way up towards the pool, via one of the bush-screened paths that criss-crossed the grounds' jungly planting. Edith saw her exchange a few words with the groundsman – who seemed as respectful of her as Ayu had been haughty with him – before kneeling at the poolside just where Edith had knelt earlier, to leave a little offering there too. The old woman began to talk again but the groundsman waved her away and completed his clearing. He respected her offering however, even making a small, private gesture as he passed it. It reminded her of the rapid, barely conscious gesture she had seen Sicilians make against the evil eye.

The scent of incense began to reach Edith's seat and when she had finished her breakfast and drained the last of her astringent green tea she went, forti-fied, to examine the offering. The groundsman smiled at her defensively as he lifted his basket of sodden foliage and petals.

'*Bhuta Kala*,' he told her. 'For the spirit,' he told her. '*Hantu*.' Then he turned swiftly away as though he had said too much.

The only thing she couldn't pack was the garland of sweetly scented flowers with which she had been welcomed. She had kept it on her dressing table and it had not yet begun to turn brown. Throwing it away would have felt wrong so, before she followed her suitcase up to Ayu and the waiting buggy, she walked back to the pool and coiled the flowers neatly about the old woman's offering.

To lighten her luggage she inscribed her nearly-new

copy of her latest novel, *A Respectable Sufficiency*, to Peter.

'Would you give this to my friend who is staying here?' she asked Ayu when they'd arrived at the entrance pavilion where her car was waiting.

'Of course,' Ayu said. 'What is their name?'

'Mr John. Peter John.'

'Oh but,' Ayu began, then she faltered. Glancing to one of her occupied colleagues, she bit her lip, a bit like a reluctant child, but took the novel from Edith. Then she smiled as defensively as the groundsman had. 'I'll give it to him, Miss Chalmers. Have a good flight now. And come back soon!'

She stood on the pavilion steps to wave the car off, as she had surely been trained to do so that each visitor could glance back at a parting tableau of delicate Balinese courtesy. However Edith saw her calling something over her shoulder whereupon two of her colleagues hurried over and stared at Edith as the car pulled away.

The driver was not her usual one and seemed to have almost no English and no desire to exercise the little he had, which was a kind of mercy. He said only, '*Berhantu!*' gesturing back at the hotel. When he saw she couldn't understand he merely shrugged and asked, 'Airport?' to which she nodded.

As they neared the top of the drive they had to slow down to allow the passage of a guest out jogging with her personal trainer. To her surprise, the guest was Lucinda Yeung, barely recognizable with her hair tied back and no make-up on but infinitely more approachable. Ms Yeung spotted her and gestured excitedly for her to lower her window.

'I'm writing a piece about you for my column, Edith,' she said. 'I wish we could have spoken more. I think your novel is very interesting. Unique, in fact. I'll see you're sent an invitation to the Hong Kong festival and get you on my cable show. You're original. So unlike all the others of your generation. I think I could really make something of you.'

'Oh. Well thank you,' Edith said.

'You'll come?'

'Of course.'

'Good.' And Ms Yeung was off again, apparently outrunning her trainer.

Hong Kong, along with Adelaide, was one of the festivals to which Margaret had always longed in vain for an invitation. Edith knew she ought to go but now that she was embarked on her journey home, to her silent flat, her books and the notes for a still unwritten novel, an ageing weariness began to steal over her. With every dusty mile placed between her and the ambiguous paradise she was leaving, she framed fresh excuses and grew in certainty that exotic travel did not suit her.

OBEDIENCE

Perran was slightly late arriving because the puppy was still unused to car travel and first vomited then shat in the Land Rover on the way over. Classes took place in a barn on a remote farm a few miles inland from Zennor. Evidently used for pony classes at other times, the old building was deeply carpeted with sawdust and its inside walls were marked out with whitewashed numbers at intervals.

As always, Chris greeted the dog not the owner. 'Evening, Toffee.'

Perran pulled Toffee to heel and joined the other pupils walking in a large clockwise circle around her. The dogs varied from a ball of fluff, too young yet to do much more than follow its owner in a childish panic, to a magnificent Belgian Shepherd, forty times its size. There was a handful of clever mongrels, a Border Collie rejected for sheep training on account of an 'hysterical tail', an ancient, unexpectedly spiteful Labrador and two white lapdogs he could not place but suspected were French. The owners were as varied as the breeds. There were children dutifully attending with bewildered Christmas presents and two women, well into their sixties, who always wore gaudy fleeces and hats as though to suggest they were warmer than their wintry expressions suggested. These two had dogs who were exceptionally obedient, clearly veterans of many classes, so perhaps they only attended as a favour to Chris, to inspire and encourage.

'Toffee, heel. Good boy,' he said, remembering to keep his tone light and playful because apparently that was what puppies responded to best.

Toffee did not look like a puppy any more. Although only five months old, he was already well over twenty-five kilos and tall enough to rest his head on the kitchen table. He was a source of some guilt. Perran had always wanted a deerhound, had been fascinated by them ever since he was old enough to pore over guides to different breeds, doubly fascinated because there seemed to be none in the county, only lurchers of all shapes and coats and the occasional greyhound, retired from racing and rescued by a charity. He had watched them on the television – at Cruft's or in period dramas – and had once been allowed to pet one as it waited obediently outside the beer tent at the Royal Cornwall Show. But owning one of his own had never been possible. First his father vetoed it, buying the family a golden retriever instead, precisely, bewilderingly, because that was what other people had. Then there was Val, his wife. Val liked dogs well enough, she maintained, but they should get children out of the way first because a farmhouse was cluttered enough without both. But then children had never come along, first because money was too short and then because of his technical difficulty.

When he saw deerhound puppies advertised in *Farmer's Weekly*, he became like a man possessed. He twice found pretexts to drive out to Dartmoor to view the litter, each time feeling as guilty as he imagined a man must feel meeting a mistress. The third time he was unable to resist buying one. It cost a crazy amount, enough to pay a broccoli cutter's wages for over twenty days, but he had some cash put by in a building society from when he got lucky on a horse, money Val knew nothing about. He introduced the puppy as a charming mongrel bought for a tenner from a man at the slaughterhouse, somewhere Val never went.

'Ten quid, for *that*?' she complained.

'He says it's nearly a deerhound,' he told her. 'At least half. Maybe more. You only have to look at him. We can call him Toffee, 'cause he's so soft.'

She fought it for a while but softened when Toffee

licked her hand and fell heavily asleep against her feet, exhausted by the terrors of a first car journey. She was adamant, however, that the dog eat nothing more expensive than scraps, that it come no further into the house than the kitchen, that clearing up after it until it was housetrained was entirely his responsibility and that should it fail to be house-trained in six weeks, it was to live in the old milking parlour.

He agreed readily to all conditions in his excite-ment; the greatest triumph was still his, after all. He hid the pedigree documentation when it arrived from the Kennel Club (Toffee's real name, his secret name, was Glencoe McTavish, of which Toffee had seemed a reasonable and plausible diminutive) and took care to lose his various pocket dog encyclo-paedias in a bale of things for the parish jumble sale, to lower the chances of Val's making comparisons between the breed ideal illustrated and the dramati-cally emerging lines of their so-called mongrel. Toffee was like a disguised prince in a fairytale; sooner or later his breeding would out.

The deadline for housetraining was two weeks gone. Perran always woke first anyway, trained to farming hours since boyhood, so it was easy enough to slip down to the kitchen, mop up any accidents, plead with Toffee to try to be good next time then slip back upstairs with a large enough mug of tea to keep Val sweet and in bed while the tell-tale taint of disinfectant floor cleaner had time to disperse. Obedience classes met with no objection; he knew she was glad to have one night a week to herself.

'And halt.' All the owners halted. Half the dogs sat obediently. The other half had to be pushed down. A puppy yelped. You could always spot the puppies who would be a handful if they grew up unchecked, the monsters-in-making. It was the same with children. Everyone watched Chris expectantly. Half the fun of these classes was that you never knew what she would have you do next; jump little pony jumps, weave your dog in and out of poles, have it sit and stay while you walked to the fullest extent of the lead or even let go of the lead altogether and crossed the room, if you were showing off and your dog could do it.

He knew she was a lesbian, that she lived with a driving instructor who had cornered the market in teaching car-shy wives and widows, but that didn't mean he couldn't admire her. She was a good-looking woman, very neat, not like Val who dressed for warmth and had a horror of revealing herself. Chris showed off her trim figure by wearing jodhpurs and a tailored suede jacket. She carried a little riding crop for pointing with and tapped it against her thigh when they were performing tasks with a pattern to them.

'And weave,' tap, 'and through the tunnel,' tap, 'and halt,' tap. He liked that. She did this for love, since the tiny fee charged could barely cover costs of barn-hire and training treats, but there was a nice mystery to her because although she plainly loved dogs, she was here without one and you had no way of knowing what breed she favoured.

'So ask her,' Val said, typically, Val who could ask anyone anything. It took a woman without mystery to assume another had nothing to keep to herself.

Chris waited until she had everyone's attention and a rescue greyhound called Misty had stopped yodelling.

'Now,' she said. 'Now that we're all here . . .' That was meant for him and Perran looked suitably crestfallen, only no one was laughing. 'I think you'll all agree,' Chris went on, 'it's only right we should have a minute's silence to think about Janice.' He looked around. Everyone was hanging their heads. One of the children was even dutifully mouthing what could have been a prayer. He hung his head too, so that Toffee looked up at him and produced one of his curious cries of uncertainty and impatience that was half yawn, half whimper.

He wanted to crouch down and give him a hug only Chris was always telling off the men in the class for leaning over their dogs too much. He supposed it was love he felt for him. Because of the lack of speech, love for animals was an odd affair, doomed to frustration. You couldn't hug them as hard as you wanted or they'd be frightened. What you really wanted, he supposed, was to *become* them. You wanted to see out of their eyes and have them see out of yours. There was a bit of particularly soft fur, just behind Toffee's huge black ears, that gave out a marvellous scent, a warm, brown biscuity smell, a bit like horse sweat, which brought on this feeling in a rush. He had heard Val talk with friends about babies often enough, heard, with an alien's fascination, how often women were filled with a hot desire to eat them, had once even seen a woman thrust one of her baby's feet entirely into her mouth and suck it. Perhaps this love of dogs and love of babies were not so dissimilar?

'So long, Janice,' Chris said at last. 'We'll miss you, girl.' Someone blew their nose. 'Now,' Chris went on, having cleared her throat. 'The police have asked if they can have a brief word with each of us afterwards. Don't worry if you'll be in a hurry. The sergeant can just take your details and pay a house call tomorrow or whatever. Otherwise they'll want statements tonight.'

'But I thought she was on holiday,' one of the elderly fleece ladies said.

'Were we the last to see her alive, then?' asked her friend.

'Looks like it.'

The greyhound yodelled again, breaking the gloomy spell.

99

'Right,' said Chris. 'Dogs are getting bored. Let's practise our downs. In a big circle now. That's it. You first, Bessie. Off you go. Not too slow. That's it. I'll tell you when. Now.'

'Down!' said Bessie's owner and Bessie dropped from her trot to flatten herself most impressively in the sawdust. It looked impressive but somehow insincere and you sensed she'd never do it so well without an audience.

So Janice was dead. Unthinkable. Janice Thomas. Haulage princess. *The Broccoli Tsarina* they had called her in The Cornishman once. Her father had begun the business in a small way, running three lorries that collected produce from the farms and took it to a wholesaler in the east. But Janice, hard-faced Janice, who nobody liked much in school, had been away to business college and made some changes when she came home. She wasn't proud. She drove one of the lorries herself for a while until she got to know all the growers, however small. Then she used her knowledge of them to persuade them to sell through her instead of merely using her as haulier, so Proveg was born, sprawling across an industrial estate outside Camborne. She was no fool. She chose the site because there was high unemployment thanks to all the closed mines and retrenching china-clay works and labour was cheap. Soon everyone had a son or daughter or wife who had done time on the packing lines or in the quality control shed. The pay wasn't brilliant but she was still regarded as something of a saviour. 'She doesn't *have* to do it,' people said. 'She could have worked anywhere. She could have worked in London for big money.'

Then she began to show her sharper side, bailing out farmers and truck owners in trouble so that she seemed their rescuer until their fortunes took enough of an upturn for them to realize that she now owned their truck or most of their farm. Or rather, that Proveg did. Janice always played a clever game of making out she was just one of the workers and speaking of Proveg as though it owned her too and she was merely another employee, paid just enough to stay loyal but never quite enough to break away.

She put her father in a home when he went peculiar – a home substantially refurbished by Proveg's charity. She drove several growers to the wall. There was a suicide or two, nothing compared to what BSE caused, but enough to register as a local outrage. Women in their cups joked that some lucky bloke would get his hands on the money soon enough but no man tamed Janice in matrimony. No woman either, for all the mutinous gossip. She lived alone in the hacienda-style estate that had sprouted from the paternal bungalow. She went to church; her pretence of worker solidarity didn't extend to attending Chapel. She smoked with defiant satisfaction. She took one holiday a year – in the brief interval between the end of the winter cauliflowers and the start of the early potatoes – always somewhere fiercely hot from where she would return with a leathery tan that showed off the gold chains that were her only visible finery. She kept a horse and bred Dobermans. She had been bringing the latest puppy to classes for several weeks now. She favoured the lean, houndlike ones rather than the overweight thugs.

When he had mentioned this, Val said, 'Lean or no, she'll never get a husband with those around the house. Devil dogs, they are.'

'Maybe she doesn't want one,' he said. 'A husband, I mean. Maybe she's happy as she is.'

'Happy? Her?' Val asked and snorted in the way she did when she wanted to imply that there were some things only a woman could understand.

'Toffee, heel. Good boy. That's it. Down. *Down!*'

'Don't repeat your order,' Chris said, as he knew she would. 'He'll just learn to ignore you.' But Toffee went down after a fashion, largely because he was tired.

'Good boy,' Perran said, then tugged him back onto his feet. 'Toffee, heel. Good boy.'

Val set great store by marriage. She thought he couldn't understand or wasn't interested, but he could tell. He saw how she divided women into sheep and goats with marriage the fiery divide between them. Women who lived with a man

102

without marrying him first she thought not loose but foolish. She did not despise spinsters or think them sad, not out loud at least, but it was plain she thought of them as lesser beings. Childlessness, her childlessness, was thus a great wound in her self-esteem. He could tell from the way she huffed and puffed over the young mothers in the village who sometimes blocked its one stretch of pavement with their double-occupancy pushchairs.

'As if they're something really special,' she snorted but her glare would have a kind of hunger to it.

He did not mind staying on to give a statement. He was collecting Val from the First and Last and she wouldn't thank him for appearing early and cramping her style. He gave his name and recognized the sergeant from schooldays. Garth Tresawle. A mate's younger brother, forever trailing behind them as they skived off, whining wait for me. And they'd had to wait because even then he had a tendency to take notes and bear witness.

'And when did you last see Ms Thomas?'

'Here,' Perran said. 'Last time we had a class. We talked a bit about boarding kennels because she was about to go on holiday to Morocco. The next day, she said.'

'You drove straight home afterwards?'

'Not exactly. I stopped off at the pub to pick up my wife.'

'What time was that?'

'Nearly closing time. Only she wasn't there. Found out later some friends had taken her on to theirs. Someone's birthday. I went back on my own.'

'Talk to anyone at the pub?'

'Er . . .' He cast his mind back to smoke, music, turned backs around the television. 'No.'

'Did anyone see you get back?'

'No. There's just the two of us and I was asleep when Val got back.' He remembered her drunken curses as she stubbed a toe on one of the bed's sticking-out legs.

'What time was that?'

'I was asleep. Past midnight.'

'How well did you know Ms Thomas?'

'We were at school together. You remember that, Garth. You were there too.'

'Sorry, Perran,' Garth sighed. 'We have to do this by the book.'

'Okay. Sorry.' Toffee whined and Perran settled him back on the sawdust. The wind was rising again, whistling round the barn roof and flapping a loosened tab of corrugated steel. 'I was at school with her so you could say I'd known her all my life, but we weren't friends. Of course I had dealings with her later, through Proveg. She buys . . . I mean she bought our broccoli and crispers. Pushed a hard bargain. Did with everyone. She won't have many friends, I reckon.'

'You harvest your own broccoli?'

'Yeah.'

'What with?'

'Knives. Same as everyone else.'

'Stainless steel?'

'No. Proveg have been on at us to change. New rules. Supermarkets don't want rust on their precious broccoli stalks. But there's nothing wrong with the old ones if you look after them. Dry and oil them. Keep them sharp with an angle grinder. And they're not brittle. The stainless ones get chipped on all the stones.'

He had been cutting broccoli since he was twelve, and in that time had seen the move from boxing them up in hessian-lined wooden crates that were taken to Penzance Station on a trailer to bagging them individually and arranging them in supermarket crates on the spot. There were health and safety regulations now. Knives had to be signed out and in by the cutters and so did any (regulation blue) sticking plasters, for fear someone get a nasty shock of finding a bloody bandage in their cauliflower cheese. Other Proveg rules forbidding smoking, eating or dogs and insisting that *in the absence of a chemical toilet, allowable where teams number five or less, antiseptic wet wipes are to be handed out to workers needing to relieve themselves in the field* he and Val blithely ignored. They had even discovered that, once the tractor had driven down a row once or twice so that tracks were well cut into the mud, it was possible to send the tractor slowly through the field without a driver, thus freeing up an extra pair of hands to cut while Val rode in the makeshift rig at the back trimming, bagging and packing. Health and safety regs would surely have outlawed this but Val kept a weather eye open and if she saw a Proveg four-wheel-drive in the distance could tip him the wink to down knife and drive for a while.

Garth Tresawle made an extra note and underlined it. He looked up.

'How many do you have?' he asked.

'Four.'

'Where d'you keep them?'

'In a shed. And no. It isn't locked.'

'How many men work for you?'

'On the broccoli?' Garth nodded. 'Two. Ernest Penrose and Peter Newson.' He gave their addresses, as best as he could remember them, and his own, and that was all.

They would have a hard time pinning charges on the mere basis of a knife. West Penwith was bristling with knives at this time of year. The daffodil and broccoli harvests brought crowds of itinerant workers into the area in search of hard labour and tax-free bundles of earthy notes. There was some resentment among the local hands, jobs being scarce, but Eastern Europeans would always be prepared to work for that little bit less than Cornishmen, especially with the threat of deportation hanging over them. Every winter there was a flurry of lightning raids by customs officers and police, tipped off about the latest troupe of illegal immigrants slaving in the eerily weedless bulb fields or in stinking acres of vegetable but every spring brought fresh vanloads. Many of them slept rough in barns and hedges to save money. Perran had found them in his sheds occasionally, or evidence of their passing through.

It was said that many of the home-grown cutters were fresh out of prison or dodging parole. He had seen the way Val discreetly clicked down the locks on the car doors when she rounded a corner at dusk to find a gang spilling across a lane, their shapes bulked out with extra clothing, their muddy knives flashing as the headlamps swept across them. There was no lack of suspicious and appropriately armed strangers to pin a local murder on.

As always, Toffee was too exhausted by the class even to remember to be carsick on the way home. Perran left him in the Land Rover while he went inside the pub.

It was a ladies' darts match night – Val played on the pub team – so there was a scattering of unfamiliar faces, though not half as many as during the tourist season. Then everyone staying on the windswept campsite would take refuge in here until closing time forced them back to caravan and canvas.

There was, however, an unmistakable holiday atmosphere tonight. He would have expected to find the women in one room, garrulous around a table, the men hunched, wordless, around Sky Sports in the other. Instead, he found the outsize television neglected and almost everyone squeezed around two long tables beside the fire, a jumble of glasses, exploded crisp packets and overflowing ashtrays in their midst. The landlady was with them, sure sign of a rare celebration, like the occasions – cup finals, the occasional wake – when she locked the doors and declared the gathering a perfectly legal private party. Ordinarily sat amongst her cronies, women she had known since childhood, Val would only have acknowledged him to demand he bought the next round or a packet of cigarettes. She certainly would not have asked him to join them but would expect him to wait with the men until she was ready to leave.

Tonight was quite different. She spotted him at once and called out, 'Here he is,' with something like eagerness. A drink was bought him and space made on the settle beside her. It was quite as though they had all been waiting for him. Someone asked how the puppy classes were going and he told her but quickly realized no one was really interested.

Then Val said, 'Well?' and it transpired that they had heard the police were questioning everyone at the class because Garth and a couple of detectives had been in the pub at the beginning of the evening and one of the detectives, the younger one with the funny eye, was a cousin by marriage of the land-lady. It was not like on television, where the facts of a murder were kept under wraps so as not to influence key witnesses. Correct police procedure was near impossible in a community this small and inter-related. They might have thought they were withholding crucial details but the women who had found the body, or most of it, Proveg employees on the night shift, were cousins of a woman on the visiting darts team and, in any case, had been far too traumatized by their discovery not to phone at least two people each before the police arrived on the scene.

Janice had been stabbed in the stomach repeatedly with a cauliflower knife. This last detail was a fair guess, given the width of the wounds the less squeamish of the witnesses had glimpsed on lifting Janice's shirt. There was no blood on the floor, so presumably she had been killed elsewhere. Her mouth had been stuffed to overflowing with cauliflower florets and a Proveg Cornish Giant Cauliflower bag strapped over her head. Her hands and arms had been hacked off. The girls could find no trace of them but, hours later, there were horrified phone calls from branches of Tesco's, Sainsbury's, Safeway's and the Co-Op where they had arrived, neatly tucked into trays of Proveg quality assured produce. And the body was said not to be *fresh* so the landlady, something of an expert on serial murder, was backing the theory that Janice had never been on holiday at all. No one knew what had become of the Dobermans or the horse but Perran asking that gave rise to a small wave of horror-struck and morbidly inventive suggestions.

'Still,' Val put in, barely keeping the relish from her voice. 'At least it looks as though they didn't suffocate her. She must have been dead already when they put the stuff in her mouth because there was no sign of a struggle. Judy said the florets weren't broken at all. Still fit to cook, she said. So what did they ask you, love?'

'Oh.' Perran shrugged. 'How long I'd known her. If we talked at the class that night – which we did, of course. What time I got home. What kind of knives we use.'

'Reckon Garth thinks you did it, boy,' someone put in. Laughter faded quickly into uneasiness.

'Well,' Perran admitted. 'I don't have a whatsit. An alibi.'

'You do!' Val insisted.

'Hardly,' he told her. 'You were out when I got home and drunk when you finally made it in.'

There was uproarious laughter at that then one of the women said, 'Maybe Val did it. She always had it in for that bitch.'

'Val had an alibi. She was with us.'

'Not like Perran. Who'd have thought it!'

'Ooh, Perran! Here, Val. You sure you're safe going home with him and everything?'

'Good on you, boy. She had it coming.'

There was teasing and laughter and, amazingly, Val clutched his thigh under the table as she laughed back and faked girlish terror. Perran felt an unfamiliar sensation as the teasing and backslapping continued and the conversation turned to Proveg and how the growers might now join forces to buy it and run it as a co-operative, which is what they should have done all along. It took a minute or two for him to identify it as pride. He had not felt like this since their wedding day.

'She'll stop,' he thought, 'once we're alone. Once we're back outside.'

And certainly Val seemed sobered by the night chill and the silence in the Land Rover. But as he drove her back to the farm, she slipped her hand over his where it rested on the gear stick.

'Poor Janice, though,' she said. 'I mean, I know she was a cow but the thought of her all alone . . . Things like that don't happen to married women. Not so often, anyway. I'm glad there's you. You too, Muttface,' she added because Toffee had woken and was leaning over from the back, sniffing the smoke in her hair. 'I'm glad there's you too. You'll keep us safe, won't you, boy?'

'Reckon he'd just wag his tail and lick the blood off the mad axeman's fingers,' he said.

'Don't!' she squeaked and shuddered.

They drove the few minutes home in silence but when he pulled up inside the garage and cut the engine she turned to him in the darkness and asked, 'You didn't do it. Did you?' And from something in her voice he sensed the distinct possibility of sex.

IN THE CAMP

Lara could normally spot the new children a mile off because they tended to cling either to their parents or to some token articles of clothing – swimming trunks, typically, but one new arrival had memorably retained long socks and sandals. But he approached them directly, as unencumbered by textiles or relatives as any regular in their little gang. Lara had not noticed until then that that summer they were all black- or brown-haired; they tended to become so muddy and stuck with leaves and twigs that such physical niceties could be hard to distinguish. He strode confidently into their midst in the forest clearing and they instinctively formed a respectful circle about him.

He was blond – real, golden blond – and his skin had the even tan of a committed naturist. Lara guessed he was twelve or even thirteen. He was just starting to grow pubic hair – she was eleven so pubic hair had begun to fascinate her – which was as golden as the hair on his head, but he still had the leanness and thin arms of a boy. He looked like the illustration of Narcissus in her book of Greek myths, only Narcissus wore a skimpy sky-blue tunic with a Greek key design and carried a bow and arrows. This boy was beautiful, she decided, and rather frightening.

'Hello,' he told them. 'I'm Wolf.' He pronounced it Volff but otherwise his English was excellent. 'What are you doing?'

'We were playing rounders,' Lara told him.

'You were pitching the ball wrong,' he told her. 'If you throw the ball underarm like that it's too easy to hit. Let me show you how to pitch properly.' He held out his hand for the tennis ball.

'I'm Lara,' she said as she handed it to him.

'Hello Lara,' he said and enslaved her with a quick, dazzling smile. 'Now watch me,' and he pitched the ball with such ferocious speed that Chubby Eric jumped aside to avoid it and tripped, which made everyone laugh. It was a bloodless coup. They had been a muddy democracy of sorts but from that moment Wolf was in charge.

He showed them how to pitch and how to strike and the game became fiercer and more exciting and a couple of children, including Chubby Eric, didn't want to play any more and slipped away, un-lamented, to find their parents. Then Wolf taught them Ball He and they chased each other back and forth between the trees, scratching their skin and bruising themselves as they slipped on the mossy patches. In fact they played He often – it was one of the best ways of keeping warm when naked as, unlike some games, it kept everybody in motion. But Ball He had an edge to it since whoever was He didn't have to get close enough to their prey to touch them but simply had to hit them with the ball. Now that Wolf had taught them how to throw, to make even a fluffy tennis ball like a bullet from a gun, their throws were more accurate and quite painful, more to be feared than a playful tap from a friend's fingers.

Lara dreaded being hit. The ball had become wet and muddy and she saw how it was leaving splatter marks on its targets that made the game more than ever like shooting. She was a swift runner and as nimble as a whippet at changing direction on her summer-toughened feet. She dodged several attacks, including one from Wolf, who shouted something in his own language when he missed her and had to retrieve the ball from the undergrowth.

At the same time she found she longed to be He, longed to be at once victim and aggressor, so she lingered on purpose, taunting him, skipping from side to side then ran in a straight line precisely so he would hit her at last. The blow stung and she felt a great spatter of cold mud it sent across her back, but now she was He and had the power she found she was laughing so hard she could barely run. She'd chased Wolf for a while but then crossed the path of Eileen, an older girl she had never much liked, and threw the ball hard at her head and darted away laughing with Wolf and the others, as Eileen cursed and slithered after the ball in the mud.

Eileen was a bad throw and, possibly on purpose, threw one of her next attempts so that the ball flew out into the lake. People moaned and said she was a spaz but, as it happened, retrieving the ball gave them all a chance to let the furious game dissolve in a leisurely swim out to the pontoon where they all flopped, panting in the sun like so many pink and brown seals.

Families dressed in the evening. It would have been too cold to stay naked but Lara suspected it also had to do with hot gravy and knives and forks. Supper was served in a big chalet beside the lake and they all sat apart with their respective families. Then there was dancing to records or a lecture but Lara usually pretended to be tired so she could go to bed with a book instead. Her parents quizzed her about the new family and seemed reassured to hear Wolf had said they were from Zurich.

'Swiss,' her mother said. 'I was sure they must be.'

Wolf's parents were just as blond as he was. They

must have been the same age as her parents nearly but they seemed far fitter. Her parents were both academics, grave and pale, helpless without spectacles whereas Wolf's parents had muscles and looked like an advertisement for something to do with health and the outdoors.

The next day her parents played them at badminton and, after dark, at bridge, so her mother must have decided they were *All Right*. Without clothes on one had to be more circumspect, apparently.

Lara knew he was a bit older than her but had thought Wolf would take his cue from their parents and become her new friend. Something about the way he had touched her arms when showing her how to pitch and caught her eye and laughed when she hit Eileen on the head made her wake fully prepared to insult or cold-shoulder whatever playmates she needed in order to cement an alliance with him. But, after two days of childish company, he suddenly seemed more interested in Mr Johnson, or Johnson, as he called him imperiously.

The Johnsons were the youngest couple in the camp. She was expecting a baby so wasn't available for games so Mr Johnson, who was dark and handsome and worked as a PE instructor in a minor public school, was much in demand.

Wolf needed to challenge him, for some reason, or at least to win his notice.

'Race me across the lake, Johnson!' he shouted

at him. 'Watch me dive, Johnson!' 'Johnson, how is my serve?'

Mr Johnson was polite and obliging. He raced Wolf and Lara across the lake, easily beating them but complimenting them on their strokes all the same and showing Wolf how to splash less with his legs. He patiently watched Wolf's repeated dives off the high board and spent some time helping him improve his tennis serve too but Lara could see he was uncomfortable, embarrassed even, at the Swiss boy's bids for attention and she wasn't surprised when he rowed his wife out to the Island after lunch. This was the one place children weren't allowed and heavy with lurid mythology as a result.

Wolf took control of the afternoon games as he had on the first two days. They played Masters and Slaves on the obstacle course and Vampires on the old tyres that dangled on ropes across the stream, but she could see, from the edge of spite that came into his commands, that he was unhappy. She still thought he was beautiful and she easily stayed on the right side of him by doing his every bidding faster and more tidily than the others so that he started calling her Tiger Cub, which she liked and hoped was a name that might stick. She had not forgotten, however, his odd foolishness in the morning and held back a part of herself in watchfulness.

She fought genuine sleepiness after supper because

there were charades that night. The Johnsons shone unexpectedly at the game, even pregnant Mrs Johnson, who was inclined to laugh too hard and get sweaty. Wolf's family proved hopeless, either through insufficient informal English or a failure to understand that the game was meant to be amusing. Her parents were neither good nor bad, which was a relief.

The next day it poured with rain. Several families donned clothes and drove off on *cultural excursions*, which would almost certainly involve the cinema, an entertainment the camp owners were far too principled to provide. Lara's parents both retreated into books. She had almost finished her last one and needed to eke it out over several more nights so she joined a raggle-taggle band of children in the games chalet for ping-pong. Interestingly most had opted to stay naked though one or two, Lara included, appeared in clothes because of the cold but soon discarded them on the chalet's old sofas and chairs so as to fit in. One boy retained just a Pacamac. More fancy dress than proper clothing, it whirled about him as he ran and began to stick weirdly to his skin where he got hot.

Sitting out a game or two with Wolf, she found he was no less interested in Mr Johnson still but that now his thoughts had turned dark with obscure disappointment.

'That Johnson is a bad sort,' he pronounced.

'How do you mean?' she asked.

'He's a pervert.'

'No!' Lara liked Mr Johnson and his funny, pink wife.

'He stares too much. He was watching you girls in the water yesterday and he touched himself when he thought no one could see him. But I saw and that's why he's avoiding me.'

'No he didn't. I expect he just had an itch. I've had itches. There are water fleas in the lake sometimes.'

'You're too young, Tiger Cub. You don't understand. He's bad. You should be careful around him.' Wolf looked less attractive when he frowned and she looked away and picked an oak leaf from between her toes.

She had said hello to Mr Johnson on her way over from her parents' cabin. He was defying the rain, heading for the woods with his binoculars slung around his neck and his bird book protected by a plastic bag. Perhaps he and his wife had *had words* and she wanted to be alone because of her heavy pregnancy. He looked a little sad, she thought, venturing off on his own and she would have offered to join him on his expedition only she had stupidly put clothes on and they were rapidly getting wet. When she grew up, she decided, a man like Mr Johnson would make a better companion than one like Wolf or his advertisement-shiny father.

Bored of sitting out, Wolf initiated a game of Round the Table. Lara enjoyed this because she was fairly hopeless at ping-pong but deft at snatching up and slamming down the bat when it was her turn to hit the ball. She liked the permitted violence of it.

The mood became wilder and wilder as more and more players were eliminated. Chubby Eric's spectacles steamed up so much he had to beg for a pause while he rubbed them on someone's discarded shirt and Eileen cracked a fingernail painfully when slamming down the racket and said fuck which induced near-hysteria. Lara was soon out too but didn't mind because another round would soon be starting.

Then Wolf, who had made it into the last four, was run out and he protested ridiculously. Everyone remembered how odd and silly he had been with all his showing off to Mr Johnson that morning and the older ones turned on him.

'Well go if you're going,' Eileen said and everybody laughed because her fuck had earned her new popularity. Even Lara laughed, because it was quite funny even though she didn't care for Eileen, and Wolf saw as he left and his eyes slid over her in a dismissive way that stopped the laughter in her throat.

When they all gathered for supper that night, Lara discovered the Johnsons had left suddenly.

Spirits were high on account of the way the weather had shaken up camp routines so there was skittish socializing between tables and word soon got around that they had been *asked to go*. *Asked to go* was the phrase always used when there had been a complaint – invariably against a man – involving staring, cameras or what Lara's mother tantalizingly called *unwonted attentions*.

Wolf ate with his parents at their usual table near the door. Nobody was gossiping with them and they were talking little to each other. Lara guessed Wolf had said something to his family during the spite-hungry tedium of the long, wet afternoon, which led to an official complaint. She was shocked to the core that he could do something so wicked and wondered if he was regretting it. Nobody liked a tell-tale.

There was a lecture that night – a woman with an unfortunately high voice talking about Birds of the Cevennes – and only scant attention was paid. Lara stayed up for once and could sense a barely suppressed excitement among the adults. Sure enough, as soon as it was seen Wolf's family had left the chalet, a kind of unofficial party broke out, with dancing and drinks, and she was hurried off to bed. Her parents returned in unusually high spirits much later than they normally did. Her mother was actually giggling and Lara enjoyed lying in her bed and eavesdropping through the curtain while they thought she slept.

124

When he tried to join them the next day, the children ignored Wolf entirely, by common, unspoken consent. The first girl he addressed directly was the newly popular Eileen, who dared to look right through him and acted as though no one had spoken. At once this became the first of the day's games and everyone followed suit. He was swiftly maddened by it, as they sensed he would be, and punched Chubby Eric hard on the shoulder. When even Chubby Eric heroically contrived to ignore his presence, he stalked off, shouting at them in his own language.

The sun returned with full heat at last and they spent the day swimming and basking, enjoying the woods and water with none of their recent savagery.

Wolf and his parents were asked to leave too. Perhaps because it involved a child their own children had been playing with, this news was kept back by most of the parents for much of the evening but inevitably it leaked out because there was nothing more interesting to discuss over supper.

In a thrilling development like something out of John Buchan, Mr Johnson had cleared his name by returning with an old army friend who was now in the Dorset constabulary. He had him challenge and question Wolf and his family before the camp owners. Wolf had refused to admit he was lying but in his ever-wilder accusations had let slip something about his father's cameras.

Bringing a camera to the camp was as strictly against the rules as men without wives. It transpired Wolf's father had not only been busy taking surreptitious snaps of them all but that his wife had been carrying a concealed cine camera in her cunningly modified knitting bag. All film was confiscated and exposed and, in a final, glorious flourish, the policeman friend had insisted on inspecting their passports before the family was escorted off the grounds.

'Germans after all,' Lara's mother said when she thought Lara wasn't listening. 'I told you I didn't really care for her.'

THE DARK CUTTER

He crossed two fields, opening the gates wide as he went, then clambered onto a hedge, cupped his hands on either side of his mouth and called.

They each had a slightly different cattle call. His older brother produced a low, booming sound midway between a moo and a foghorn. Their father's call had two notes, the second lower than the first, and usually had a trace of words to it, a sort of weary 'come 'long'. His own tended to emerge as a sort of falsely cheery *Hey-oop!* with a rising note at the end. He hated raising his voice or trying in any way to seem different but, try as he might to imitate the others, his call always came out the same way.

Fog had come in off the sea soon after dawn and was drifting inland as a succession of clammy curtains. The steers were Charolais crosses so in these conditions became almost invisible, their buff and off-white flanks barely distinguishable from the pale granite of the hedges and pearly grey of the fog. There was a distant low-lying field where they spent the night sometimes, grouped together out of the wind like so many companionable boulders. He was about to jump off the hedge to go in search of them there when he heard them – one crazily high-pitched moo first and then a chorus of baritone answers – and stayed put to call them again. There was another moo, closer at hand, before their great forms lumbered out of the surrounding grey.

They were following one of their leaders, a burly, roundshouldered animal, whose lopsided horns had been sawn off a few months back when one threatened to grow into its cheek.

He slid down off the hedge and, calling them again, waited until a few had come close enough to sniff and recognize him then began to lead them back the way he had come, across the fields to the lower yard. The trick was to walk slowly enough to hold their interest but with enough speed to keep them from merely falling to graze on a different acre. Luckily the herd had been in this run of fields for ten days now and was eager for change.

As he walked, he heard their snorting breaths and felt the ground shake whenever one of them gambolled up a yard or two to his side. Occasionally, driven by an overflow of energy perhaps, one would mount another and ride it for a yard or two or a couple would suddenly pair off for a quick trial of strength, thumping their huge skulls together, eyeball to eyeball, fringe to fringe, then pushing until one yielded to the other. All about him now, they gave off what he thought of as their smell of contentment – a yeasty mixture of the sharp-sweetness of chewed grass with the sweaty tang of their pelts.

He slipped back to close a gate behind them as the last stragglers passed through then hurried forward with a shout to encourage the herd to keep up its momentum. Seven times out of ten they came like this when called, not from obedience – he knew better than to credit them with that – but from hunger, curiosity or boredom. The other times, when they refused to come but simply ran in maddening circles or, worse, lay unbudgeably munching, tended to arise when the field they were in was still fairly new to them.

Who was he kidding? There was no order or method to these creatures; sometimes they were cussed or flighty, sometimes they weren't.

Inspired, perhaps, by the dawning realization that they were nearing the farmyard, where they were fed barley in season, and the familiar Dutch barn where they were bedded down in the coldest, wettest weeks of winter, one of the steers suddenly kicked up its heels and broke into an ungainly, farting run, taking the others with it. They surged through the second gate and he raced to shut it after them. As he secured it with a length of old barbed wire he grazed the inside of his wrist and swore softly.

The herd was swallowed by a fresh veil of fog as it rounded the awkward corner above the farm-yard. The hope was that his father and brother were ready for it with open gates and an open pen so the steers could pass straight to their destination. Sometimes some small thing, a laughing child, a darting cat, a fertilizer bag caught and flapping on the gorse, would panic them at the crucial moment and send them skittering back in a way that would be comical if it weren't so irritating. An angry half-hour or more could follow in which they attempted to round the herd back towards the yards in an L-shaped field with all too many awkward corners where they could baulk and huddle. He wished at such times that they possessed a cattle dog. Not a spooky border collie, with those staring eyes, but a proper cattle dog, reliable and sturdy, like the ones Australians used, to help round the beasts back towards the yard. But his father hated dogs, having been mauled on the hand as a boy, so the wish was futile, at least while the old man lived.

This morning they were lucky and the beasts ran, unstartled, into the main yard and down to the lower one where they could be sorted. The lower yard gate, a far heavier one than those they had passed in the fields and with proper fastenings, was clanged shut behind them. He then had to join his father and brother in trying to persuade the herd into the big pen.

Like many parts of the farm, the lower yard had evolved by a subtle interplay of accident and necessity in which design had played little part. It was an L-shape, or a V, even, with gates top and bottom and pen and crush off at the farthest end. There was also a marked change in level where the yard turned a corner.

As usual his brother had parked one of the tractors to block off one angle and placed a line of feeding troughs behind it so as to steer the animals towards the pen's open gate. As usual the steers ignored the hint and surged down to the other, closed, gate, pressing their faces to it to peer out at the tantalizing fresh pasture beyond. When shouted at and chased, they simply ran back uphill the way they had come. They ran back and forth a couple of times, from the top of the slope to the bottom. Growing increasingly nervous and with one or two of them slipping and falling in the rush, until enough of them led the way into the pens for the others to be fairly readily chased and whipped into following suit.

He hated whipping them. He and his brother had stiff lengths of blue plastic water pipe which extended their reach when trying to head the animals off but which were inevitably used to prod and beat as well. Their father preferred the riding crop from his hunting days, which was shorter but had a little tassel of leather on its end 'to pack a good sting', as he liked to say.

He knew this soft distaste in him was shameful and unmanly, that directing the animals firmly, with shouts and even kicks, was the only and the safest way. Yet he winced inside at the sound of whip on hide. He never whipped the face of a turning animal the way the others did and only used his hose when he was frustrated at some beast's stupidity. They all talked to the animals as they worked, saying things like, 'Get in, would you?' and 'Oh, you bloody thing!' but he suspected he was the only one of them who, in his mind at least, muttered apologies too.

As always he was the one to jump into the pen with the steers to direct them, four at a time, into the smaller pen and on to the crush. His brother would work the crush gates and neck-clamp and his father would peer into twitching ears and tick off herd and animal numbers in a muddy notebook. Being inside the pen was, he knew, the most dangerous job next to lassoing a steer's swollen foot in the crush, one where you were likely to be kicked or crushed against the bars, but he was quite unafraid so knew he could do the job without hitting them. He liked to think he could calm the animals by talking to them in a kind, low voice as he waved them through the gate between the pens or out into the crush but knew they were basically wild at heart and wanted no man near them however kind-hearted. They hated this abrupt interruption of their freedom and the replacement of grass with shitty concrete and the clamour of cold steel. The crush weighed them as they passed through it and made a terrible oily clanking. Even briefly held in place in it by the neck, they invariably shat themselves soupily with the shock of it. The sharply grassy smell of the herd in the pasture was soon replaced all about him by the sourer stench of fear.

Thirteen steers were needed for collection by the cattle lorry the next morning. The law had relaxed since the BSE crisis but they were still effectively obliged to have every animal slaughtered before it was thirty months old. One or two were obviously finished, weighing in at six hundred and fifty kilos or more and with properly beefy flanks and thighs. Others of the same age were not such good feeders and needed a few weeks more. So there was much arguing about which of the borderline cases should go. Then one of the ready ones was found to have lost his metal ear tag which won it a stay of execution because it was illegal to send them to slaughter without two tags in place, and another Hansel and Gretel discussion ensued as to who was fat enough to take the lucky animal's place.

The twelve already picked had been ushered in twos and threes to the cattleshed on release from the crush. The remaining animals now milled nervously around as they were inspected, snorting, ducking their heads, and seeking comfort in the closest possible proximity to each other. Some even thrust their heads shoulder deep between their neighbours' legs. Others pressed, head first, in tight huddles in the inner corners of the pens as if affecting an interest in the weeds on the high walls, all unaware that it was their rumps, not their faces, that were being assessed.

At last a choice was made, a stocky two-year-old that, though still giving the impression of youth because he was so much shorter than his companions, had filled out his frame as far as he was likely to do. He joined the others in the shed with something like relief, kicking up his heels as he felt himself on deep straw and out of scrutiny. The rest were turned out from the yard's lower gate into new pasture and soon broke into a run and were lost to view in the fog.

How soon did they forget? It was a question he had last dared ask thirty or forty years ago, when he was a boy and it was still profitable for their father to run a dairy herd alongside the beef one. Some calves had just been separated from their mothers and the despondent, regular lowing had kept waking him in the night.

'They're animals,' his father said. 'They don't remember. They don't understand time. They get worried sometimes but that's just instinct, not feeling. Don't let it bother you.'

But it did bother him. Frequently. And he envied friends at school whose fathers produced only daffodils and broccoli on their land, or potatoes and anemones. Growing up, he had hoped for but never acquired, the hard outer layer that had come so naturally to his brother. He mastered all the tasks that were set him. He had been on courses on chemical spraying and hedgerow management and conservation headlands. He learned how to fill out the complex paperwork that would prove they had complied with new regulations and qualified for various EU subsidies. He had even done quite well in ploughing matches over the years. He had proved he was a good judge of calves at auction. But still this inner softness, weakness even, persisted and made him feel an impostor among his family and peers.

Looking at advertisements in *Farmer's Weekly* sometimes, at the sentimental picture plates of wet-eyed calves and contented sows with titles like *Little Mischief* or *A Mother's Pride*, he wondered if he were not mistaken. Perhaps all farmers felt the way he did and were simply masking their occasional discomfort from one another, the way men liked to pretend to each other that they had neither respect for women nor emotional need of them.

137

Once, when a steer they had only had a week sickened and died, racked by seizures thought to be caused by lead paint poisoning from some shed on the farm where he was reared, his father seemed upset for a few minutes but that might simply have been because he had not put the animal down himself with a gun instead of incurring hefty vet's bills in the hope of pulling the wretched thing through.

Another time a cattle lorry had come driven by a man who started using an electric prod as they herded the steers on board and his brother had sent him away indignantly and complained to the haulier who had hired him. But that hadn't been concern for the animals' welfare so much as worry the animals would not fetch a fair price. If an animal was frightened before slaughter, he claimed, it could tense up so badly its muscles held too much blood in a way that would spoil the meat. He had simply feared that a cattle prod would tense them up more than a simple whip or stick would do. The slaughtermen called such a blood-heavy carcass a *dark cutter*, his brother told him, a term that now came back to him whenever he passed a butcher's shop window or was chopping meat for a stew.

He had topping to do all that afternoon so he could listen to the radio in the tractor as he drove up and down the grass fields for a few hours, dreaming of other places, other lives. But that evening, just before sunset, he slipped down to the shed where the cattle were waiting. If his brother had challenged him, he'd have said he was heaping up the silage for them but he also came down to exercise his guilt and wonder.

It was amazing how swiftly the mud and shit crumbled off their coats when they were bedded down in a good depth of clean straw. He stood a while, leaning on his pitchfork, watching their eyes on him as they chewed or rubbed their noses on the silage heap in a kind of ecstasy of greed. They looked healthy, content again, and, of course, entirely unsuspecting, and this cheered him. He wanted them to have as good a last night as possible and was disgusted at himself. Faced as they must have been with an occasional lovely face or particularly endearing child, had concentration camp guards indulged in a similar sick sentimentality? Had they given their charges pet names and convinced themselves their arbitrary instances of kindness counted for anything?

They had toad-in-the-hole for supper. He ate too much and slept badly, tormented by indigestion and dreams in which he must answer for himself to his father and accusing friends but could muster only bovine bellows.

They had an extra-early start, before sunrise, to be ready for the lorry. Guiding steers from their shed into a cattle truck was even harder – given their arrangement of buildings – than persuading them around the yard and into the pens. Cattle lorries were so long they would only fit into the main farmyard one way and had to be parked hard up against the cattleshed's outside wall. The animals had to make a u-turn, out of their shed, in through a smaller one that might once have been a piggery, and out through its other side where a narrow door opened directly opposite the lorry's rear. To steer them from the large shed into the smaller one, the two tractors were parked tightly, nose to tail, with a couple of pallets lashed on either end, blocking off any other route. An old galvanized steel gate was leant against the side of the lorry's tailgate to prevent escapes and help channel the animals up and in and the tailgate was thickly spread with old straw from within the small shed to mask any alien smells like pig which might have lingered from previous loads.

Cattle lorries had barriers which folded out from the walls and subdivided their interiors to stop animals falling and hurting themselves. Six or so steers at a time could be driven in and the barrier folded out and bolted shut behind them. But persuading even six animals to pass through the small door on the other side of the little shed and up into a lorry – something they had only been in once before, when they were far smaller and more biddable – could rarely be accomplished at the first attempt. Steers had a maddening way of bunching up inside the little shed, forming a bottleneck just

140

inside the door or allowing the inevitable curses and thwacks to panic them. As often as not one, placed just out of range by his brothers, would take one suspicious look at the lorry then turn around to face the wrong way, obstinately blocking the route for his fellows. Once one of them took fright and decided to run back the way they had come it was impossible to stop the others following and the shed was so low and small it would have been crazily dangerous for a man to push in there with them in an effort to head them off. All one could do was try to block the route back to the bigger shed, lashing out and cursing when the steers tried to turn back and cooing desperate encouragement at the least sign of an animal daring to pass on into the lorry. Sometimes just one or two would comply and stagger up the tailgate and in only to be spooked and thunder back down when their brothers failed to join them quickly enough.

Of all the stages of his interaction with a steer, the day of its departure was the one when his determination to treat it humanely was most likely to crumble. If only they would trot peaceably on board the way they entered a new field, it would have been possible to treat them well until the last. But they never went peaceably, or very rarely. His guilt at sending them for slaughter fed his frustration at their wilfulness and stupidity and he would lash out as fiercely as his brother then feel himself diminished for it.

The sun rose on a steady, penetrating drizzle and the lorry arrived so soon afterwards that it might have spent the night in a lay-by in the village and been waiting there for dawn. The driver was new and not local. Masking his nerves in truculence, he complained about the smallness of the yard.

'Nobody told me,' he said, although his lorry was no longer than usual, and he made a great performance of having to nose up into Home Field then execute a multiple-point turn in order to be able to back up to the position where they needed him.

No one was like this when their father was around, as he had one of those stern countenances that commanded respect, but he had driven up-country for a cousin's funeral the night before.

'I don't do rounding up,' the driver said flatly, hearing a steer bellow inside the cattleshed as he climbed down. 'No insurance.'

The farm was insured against third-party claims, it had to be. But no one told him that as it was not a thing one wanted known. The usual driver always helped a bit. He liked to. But he was a farmer's son and knew what he was about; a novice in such a situation offered more risk than assistance. This man was an outsider and an unknown quantity. He was older than most drivers and had a terse bitterness to him that spoke of failures and bad solitude.

'Just stand and hold the gate firm against the tailgate,' they told him. 'We'll do the rest.'

They could manage with just the two of them so long as the driver held his ground at least and had the sense not to start shouting and hissing at the animals as they approached.

Watched suspiciously by him, they made the last few arrangements, scattering straw and securing the barrier for him to stand behind. Then they walked in through the small shed and counted out the first six cattle.

These milled around a little at first, mooing mistrustfully and driving him and his brother back into the space between tractors and cattleshed a couple of times. Then their leader showed the way, heading up the tailgate with a few clattering steps. The rest followed him with little resistance until they felt the safety barriers being swung across and bolted behind them, by which time it was too late.

The next seven included an especially strong, wild specimen his brother had nicknamed Shakin Stevens on account of his quiff, that had once actually jumped out of the crush when being wormed, and they proved far less tractable. They surged in and out of the little shed several times, only panicked further by the stinging from the hosepipes. They wedged themselves in there the wrong way round, backs to the exit, blinking as the blows and curses rained down on their faces. They squirted diarrhoea across each other and rained down piss by the gallon. They answered the mooing from their brothers in the lorry with bellows and snorts. The stupid driver made matters worse by trying to encourage them as if he were on a rugby touchline and their curses at the cattle became as much curses at him, not that he would have noticed above the din and churning back and forth. Then one of them, who had spent several minutes blocking the exit for the others while he stared out at the lorry, finally took a step or two back and the rest began to leave. First two tried to go through at once and threatened to become wedged, then they went out in quick succession.

He and his brother pressed on into the shed hissing, shouting, waving their arms and lashing out so as to be sure the others followed before the leaders changed their minds and doubled back. The driver shouted again, even louder this time, and they cursed the bugger for his stupidity that might cost them another ten minutes of torment. Then there was a bright ding of hoof on metal and the clang of a falling gate and suddenly there was mooing coming from quite the wrong direction.

All at once the other four animals surged out.

Damning the idiot for not having even the nous to hold a leaning barrier in place, his brother stamped out after them and immediately swore and shouted for him to follow and quickly.

The last seven cattle were loose in the farmyard. Two were tasting the willows in the hedge. The rest

144

were merely standing, nonplussed by their un-expected release.

The driver lay on his back, hands flung up above his head as though he were falling down a pit. The gate he had been holding in place lay across his hips. There were muddy hoof prints up the front of his overalls, as in some cartoon. The kick that had felled him had caused his nose and a part of his forehead to cave in so that his face was now a kind of bowl where vivid blood was pooling.

He ran to the back door to ring for an ambu-lance, although he was fairly sure the man was dead, and to call the abattoir. Another driver could not be freed up until that afternoon at least, so they had to move the tractors then let out the steers that were already loaded and herd all thirteen animals back into the cattleshed. If one of them had blood on its hoof, it was impossible to tell which by now. He forked up the silage for them and they fell to eating at once, swiftly calmed by food.

It did not seem right to move the body until the ambulance arrived but they lifted the gate off it and laid the man's hands at his sides.

'We should cover it,' he said. 'Shouldn't we?' But his brother couldn't answer because he was slumped in the filthy straw on the tailgate and had buried his face in his palms, shoulders heaving.

He was fetching clean potato sacks from the mill shed to make a sort of shroud when a family of

145

walkers arrived on the footpath from the cliffs, thinking to cross the farmyard, and he felt he had to wave his arms and warn them off as they had children with them. As he shouted instructions that came out more abruptly than he'd intended because of his nerves, and sent them the long way round the farm, down the lane instead of across the fields, he saw fear in the husband's eyes and, in the wife's, something like disgust.

MAKING HAY

The children burst in full of the pleasure they assumed the young, by their very youth, gave to the old. While they were signing the visitors' book, Maudie exchanged a look with Prue then reached into the baby jacket she had been pretending to knit for some weeks. She took out a crib she kept hidden on a piece of card and scanned it expertly. *Grandchildren*, she read. *James, nine, vehicles, foot-ball, bananas. Effie, seven, ponies, death, Jaffa Cakes.* There was a number after every entry on the card, be they friend or relative, to indicate how much she currently loved them. Neither child was scoring highly.

'Look who's come to see their old granny!' she exclaimed, catching sight of her daughter-in-law's pick-up speeding away.

James and Effie kissed her dutifully. Effie sat in one of the specially high-seated armchairs and bounced self-consciously. James mooched, staring at Maudie's bandage.

'Wave hello to your grandfather.'

They waved uncertainly. Maudie's husband sat apart with the few male residents. The cramped back sitting room, where smoking was allowed, was the men's territory. They congregated, taciturn, around the sports channel for the long stretches between meals, leaving the ladies the run, so to speak, of the more spacious and sociable day room. Grandpa stared at the children blankly but two of his companions waved back and Herbert Boskenna did that clicky thing with his dentures which was his equivalent.

'Can I watch too?' James asked. 'The Grand Prix's on.'

'No, dear. The men don't like to be disturbed. Maybe when you're older.'

'How about in here, then?'

'Miss Tregenza's waiting for Gary Cooper.'

'She's asleep,' put in Effie and they all looked briefly at Miss Tregenza, a thin, pale thing with little hair and no conversation.

'No, dear,' Maudie observed. 'She always looks that way when she's waiting.'

'Nurse'll be in in a moment,' said Prue, 'to turn Gary Cooper on, then she'll perk up. You'll see. She likes Gary Cooper. We all do.' Prue gave one of the coarse chuckles which reminded Maudie why they had never been friends until now.

'There's a banana in that fruit bowl with your name on it,' she told James but the boy sulked, unused to denial. 'Do you want a Jaffa Cake, Effie?'

Effie pulled a long face. 'I'm on a diet,' she said. 'Mum says I mustn't eat between meals.'

'Well teatime's a meal.'

Effie pulled the face again. 'Better not,' she said.

'How long have you got?' Maudie asked them both.

James sighed with a characteristic want of tact. 'Quarter of an hour,' he said, as though that were a small eternity. 'She's gone to Cornwall Farmers to fetch Dad more wrapper for the silage.'

'Is he doing that this afternoon, then? I wouldn't have thought it was dry enough . . .'

'Yup,' James said absently, staring as Nurse clicked in a Gary Cooper DVD. Miss Tregenza's reanimation was nothing startling but she opened her eyes, shut her mouth and assumed a look of complacent serenity. She began to croon the introductory music, slightly in advance of the orchestra.

'Knows all the tunes,' Prue said as the titles rolled up the screen. 'Ooh, *The Fountainhead*. I think I like this one. Patricia Neal always had such lovely, crisp-looking hair.'

'Wouldn't you rather be helping your dad?' Maudie asked, ignoring her.

151

'Not really,' James said. 'It's all tractor work really. Mum won't let me load new rolls of plastic on the bale-wrapper in case I get my hands stuck.'

'Well that's the trouble with silage, isn't it Prue? All done by machine. Wrapped in plastic. No art to it at all, really.'

'Lazy, I call it,' Prue said.

'And it stinks,' said Effie. 'It's nice enough now but when you cut it open in the autumn it's like sick with mould on.'

'In our day,' Maudie told them, 'everyone round here still made hay and that doesn't stink. Good hay smells sweet.'

'What's hay?' Effie asked.

'Dried grass, stupid,' James said, watching the film.

'It's more than that,' Maudie told him. 'Hay's a craft. It's a mystery. You have to cut it just at the right time. The ears can be forming but leave it too late and there's no goodness left. And it has to be dry. You need four clear, dry days at least. You can't cut it wet 'cause it won't dry right lying down. It has to be cut dry then tedded – that's turned to you – twice daily. It has to dry fast so the goodness doesn't leach out. If you're slow drying it, respiration carries on and the sugars turn to gas and water.'

'And heat,' Prue put in. 'Hay gets hot. Put it in a rick too soon and the whole thing could go up. Every few years someone would have an almighty fire.

When we were younger, the whole family lent a hand, cousins and all. If you were old enough to walk, you were old enough to turn hay. And there were competitions.'

'There still are, for silage,' James put in. 'Dad says there's no point.'

'Nothing wrong with competitions if you've a chance of winning,' Maudie said to shut him up. 'Your grandfather, in his time, was the most competitive haymaker on this peninsula. He wasn't like the others, though, watching weather vanes and looking how high the birds were feeding; he went out and got the science. Knew all about balancing his herbage dry matter and how he had to get the moisture content down by a third.'

'A quarter,' Prue put in sharply. 'They reckon you should aim for a hundred and fifty grams per kilo nowadays.'

'If you say so,' said Maudie, who maintained a stout disapproval of metrication. 'He knew about amino-acid leaching and stomata closure and the rest. He was obsessed with raising his yields. He was sure if you prepared the grass in the right way back in the early spring, you could produce a hay that took up the same amount of space in the barn but fed the animals twice as well.'

'Didn't he have a muck spreader?'

'Of course he did but that wasn't enough.'

'What about fertilizer?'

'We couldn't afford chemicals. We had to make do with what nature gave us.'

'What, then?'

Maudie edged forward in her chair slightly, aware that she was competing for their attention with Gary Cooper. 'Blood,' she pronounced.

'Dried blood?' asked James.

'No.' She was scornful. 'That's no use. When Mother Eddy went peculiar and danced off a cliff and they cleared out her cottage, he found an old book which spelled it out for him. You needed fresh blood. There was plenty of blood when we killed a pig but we used all that for puddings. But he got chickens.'

'Not much blood in a chicken,' Prue sighed.

'It was quality that mattered. Quality and fresh-ness. And then there were the kittens.'

'No!' Effie was deeply shocked.

'Of course. Barn cats have kittens all the time. It's a fact of life. And the mothers'd die of hunger and exhaustion if you let them raise them all. My dad always used to drown them. Put them in a sack, nice and quick, and into that old cattle trough at the top of the yard. Don't be silly, Effie. It was a natural kindness. He had to do it. But then your grandfather there started taking the kittens himself. He thought I didn't know but I'd see him keeping an eye on the litter instead of drowning it straight away.'

154

'Wanted them plump and juicy,' Prue said with just the right hint of relish.

'That's right. One day he'd be out there in the barn, weighing them in his hands and the next night he'd take longer than usual shutting the yard gate and walking the dog. And I'd know what he'd been up to because he'd spend an age washing his hands. I even heard the little click as he slipped the fruit knife back into that rack by the bread crock.'

There was a pause filled only by a startled cough from Miss Tregenza as Gary Cooper's astonishing profile caught the light. Effie breathed through her mouth. The child needed her adenoids out. Maudie briefly summoned up the gratifyingly intense image, glimpsed through a slyly lifted floorboard, of her sister, Bridie, gassed and splayed on the kitchen table, having hers removed by Dr Wadsworth.

'Did it work?' James asked suddenly and his voice pulled her back from reverie.

She looked at him hard; the image of his father. In that, at least, he did not disappoint. 'Do you know, it *did*,' she said. 'At least, he took the Grassland Association's cup two years in a row. But winning wasn't enough. He'd set himself a challenge to beat.

'The third year it was a horse. I even remember his name. Destry. As in *Destry Rides Again*. He was the last of the horses. We had the first tractor west of Penzance but that wasn't until 1938. Anyway, poor Destry hadn't been put out to pasture for two months when his heart gave out. The vet said he'd had a murmur but I think it was sorrow. He missed the labour. Anyway, horses were usually shot by the knacker when their time came. He'd come out and finish them off kindly then buy what was left for dog meat. Don't look like that, James. During the war, people ate horse, too.'

'Tasty,' Prue said nostalgically. 'Red wine. Bit of juniper to take off the muskiness.'

'Horse meat, Prudence. Not dog.' Maudie shook her head to the children, as though to explain that Prue wasn't all there.

'But your grandfather said no. After all Destry had done for the farm and seeing he was the last of the line, he should do the deed himself and call the knacker out afterwards. Well, I thought. We're moving on from kittens now. And sure enough he didn't finish him off until after dark. Told Mum it was because he couldn't bear Destry to see the shotgun but I knew it was the blood. He needed to shed the blood at night so it would have plenty of time to soak into the soil before the sun rose and dried it up. And he must have known a shot to the head wouldn't reach a big enough artery so he wanted to use a knife afterwards and be able to rinse his boots and hands off under cover of darkness.' She sighed. 'Funny, though. I'd forgotten all about it when they called us all out to get the hay in that summer. But then I breathed it in.'

156

'Was it . . .' James was all attention. 'Was it disgusting like silage?'

She paused for effect. 'It was the sweetest hay I had ever smelled. Like fresh baked bread in a ripe orchard. I took one sniff and I caught your grandfather's eye – he was a very handsome man in those days – and he smiled, ever so slightly. So I knew I was right. And it didn't just win him the cup again, it was like miracle food. The cattle were so sleek and muscly on it and the meat, when it came, was so well marbled with fat, someone started a rumour we'd been doctoring them with some chemical. Which we hadn't, of course. Nothing but grass, our own milled barley and our own sweet hay.'

'Cream and roses,' sighed Miss Tregenza so suddenly even Maudie was startled.

'What's that?' Prue asked her.

'How you can tell a good bit of meat.' Miss Tregenza's eyes were momentarily freed to roam as Gary Cooper had left the scene to less principled and therefore less handsome characters. The tip of her tongue crept out to moisten thin lips. 'Puts you in mind of cream and roses.'

The sad falling off in meat quality with the rise in low-fat cookery was a pet topic of Maudie's but she had a professional eye on the clock and her fifteen minutes were nearly up. 'Anyway,' she continued, 'I thought to myself that'll be it now. He can't get another horse. He can't make sweeter hay than this. He can rest on his laurels. Sure enough he went back to letting my dad drown the barn kittens and our hay was good but no better than anyone else's who knew to watch the weather and judge the season.

'But then the War came and all the evacuees. Hundreds of grubby, rowdy little town children on the trains from Paddington and Bristol. Some of them had never seen the sea before, never mind a cow. We had six – four boys and two girls – *and* those saucy Land Girls. But one of the six children went missing. A little tyke, he was. Red hair, crusty knees, hated washing. About your size and age,' she said, carefully assessing James. 'Jacky. Jacky Porter. No one was surprised when he vanished. He was forever wandering, always skiving off when they were walking to school. So we just supposed he'd run off back to London. We did all we could. The sad thing was that he went just too early to find out he'd nowhere to run *to*. Mother and aunt dead in a flattened house. Terrible really. And he had no father who'd claim him.'

'Shame,' Prue sighed and shook her head at the fecklessness of men. The children only stared. Maudie pretended an interest in the progress of the baby jacket.

'That summer,' she said, 'when your grandfather had cut the hay and the girls and I were out tedding it, I came across a Fair Isle cardigan. Well I knew it had belonged to the Porter boy but I thought nothing of it. He was a tearaway who left clothes all over the place and, as often as not, had a sock missing or couldn't find his tie before church. But I gave it to your granddad to hand in to the police, just in case. And there was something in his face as I passed it to him. A sadness. A kind of . . . dignified regret.

'I've often wondered what he did with the body. Down one of the old mineshafts? Or perhaps he ploughed it into a barley field.'

'What about the hay?' Effie asked impatiently.

'Hang on a second, dear. Knit two, purl two, cast one onto t'other, knit two, purl two . . . The hay? The hay had no smell at all. Looked fine enough. Dried quick enough. But it was a dead thing. Characterless. And I swear to God the cattle didn't like it and we actually had to buy in bales from Zack Hosking. And if the story ended there, I'd have said it was divine punishment, plain and simple and that he saw the error of his ways.'

'Why?' James asked. 'Did the grass die?'

'Lord, no. It takes more than a bit of blood to kill off a whole field of grass. It was stranger than that. We let the cattle in the field for a few weeks that autumn before the rains started in earnest and I went up there one morning to check they had enough water. And they were nosing at something. You know how inquisitive steers get? They were nosing and dragging their hooves. So I walked through them to take a look and there was a sort of mound. Like a big molehill. Well we don't get any moles, as you know. Only rabbits. So I thought it was a bit queer and I scraped a bit at the earth with my toe, the way the cattle had started to. And they were all nosing around me and snorting and sneezing.' Maudie mustered a shudder. 'I remember it so clearly. I crouched to feel and my fingers found a sort of . . . well *skin*, really. Greyish, where the earth had been on it, but pink inside and quite warm. Well, I dug more aside and realized it was a sort of . . . a sort of *bag*. Full of liquid and . . . and something else. I was just going to run and fetch your grandfather or one of the Land Girls – they were only a few fields away – when it kicked. Or something inside it kicked.

'Prudence, it's no good. You're going to have to finish this matinée jacket for me – I can't make head or tail of this blinking pattern.

'You know how sometimes you go into a house or into a room and, although you can't say exactly what's wrong, you get a bad feeling?'

Both children nodded although it was certain neither had the slightest psychic ability. Even Prue had fallen quiet. The only sound was Nurse using the rotary iron in the hall, the murmur of sports commentary from the smoking room and subdued, manly conversation from Gary Cooper and a colleague.

160

'Well that's how I felt and I sensed that what-ever it was, I had to destroy it. I ran to the hedge and fetched the biggest bit of granite I could carry and heaved it back. I thought I'd just shut my eyes and drop it on the thing, the way you would on a rabbit with myxomatosis. I wasn't thinking beyond that, of the mess or having to explain it or anything. I was just about to let go when I heard a strange sucking, whiny sound, a bit like a very new kitten now I think of it. And I opened my eyes, looked down and almost dropped the rock.

'The skin of the bag, or whatever it was, had sort of split apart and there, all wet and shiny like a little seal was a baby. A perfect, black-haired boy baby. The skin had shrunk up like a burst balloon but the last of it was sticking to his head and, as I bent to scrape it off him, he opened his soft blue eyes, emptied the stuff out of his mouth and claimed me with his cry as surely as if he had called me Mother.'

Maudie glimpsed her daughter-in-law's returning Jeep. 'And that,' she said, 'was the baby that grew into your father.'

There was a stunned silence.

'I don't believe it,' James said at last.

'*I* don't care,' Maudie told him. 'He'd deny it, of course, because it's only human to want to be like everyone else. I just thought you ought to know. That's why his middle name is Fielding.'

'The mark,' Effie said softly, remembering something. 'There's a red mark on his head where his hair's falling out. Is that . . .?'

'Yes, dear. Where the bag was stuck to him. His birthmark, if you like. Now here's your dear mum to take you home.'

They were curiously reluctant to leave but more reluctant still to do as their mother bid them and hurry next door to give Grandpa a fond goodbye kiss. Herbert Boskenna clicked his teeth at Effie while she was waiting her turn and the child truly turned pale with fear.

'She ought to eat more,' Maudie told her daughter-in-law, 'and he needs to watch less television – it's giving him nightmares. Bye all. Come back soon.'

'The trick,' she confided in Prue as Nurse wheeled in the tea things and wheeled out Miss Tregenza, 'is to spike the narrative with just a seasoning of solid, agricultural fact.'

BRAHMS AND MOONSHINE

The clouds had drifted away during the concert and people exclaimed, as they emerged from the church, at the unexpected brightness of the moon and stars. A comet was making a centennial appearance in the western sky that Easter. Gretel wanted to linger with the others to admire the clarity of its tail but Corey was keen to be off. The Requiem had barely begun when he realized each of them had supposed the other had shut the chickens in their coop before leaving. He had been fretting about foxes ever since.

'Isn't it beautiful?' she said, meaning the comet. Her heart was still brimming with Brahms and she wanted to make the rare sensation last.

'Yes, come on,' he said. 'If we get a move on we can get out of there before we get stuck in a queue with this lot.'

She followed him obediently, feeling in her wallet for the key to the van. There was a retiring collection after the concert to assist the fine old church's restoration. Still blissed-out on music, Gretel had reached for her money as they left their pew, generosity welling up within her, only to find he had raided her funds to buy oil for the chainsaw. She could offer nothing to the pretty girl with the begging bowl but twenty pence and a worthless, craven smile.

The concert-goers' cars were crammed into a field across from the church. It had been drizzling all week. She felt cold mud on her toes as she hurried after him and cursed the foolish impulse which had prompted her to wear pretty shoes and her least ancient dress. No one else had dressed up; forewarned, they thought only of warm practicality. The exceptions were the musicians, glimpsed here and there, incongruous in backless dresses or dinner jackets amid the mud and four-wheel-drives.

The van was not a four-wheel-drive but an old, much-patched Commer converted to a mobile home, built for unhurried journeys and long, recuperative rests. When they arrived, she had taken one despairing glance at the mud and pleaded with the young musician waving them in to let her park on the thin island of firmer ground near the entrance. But he was bound by regulations and insisted, smiling, that she park with the other large vehicles, most of them shamingly new and all of them surely better equipped for such conditions.

'Well go on, then.'

'We're skidding.' She felt the sickening lack of grip.

'Slowly,' Corey said, 'or you'll make it worse. Ease her out. Steady!'

She drove because he had lost his licence before he met her. Some terrible tale involving a child, a bicycle and worn brake shoes. Told her in the flush of new love, the story had demanded and won her sympathy but increasingly its lack of details came to rankle and her mind framed the questions she could never ask. What was the child's name? How old? Just how badly disabled had the accident left it? And why did Corey only voice indignation, not remorse?

'Here. Let me. There's a tarp back there. Stick it under the wheels with that old blanket and I'll try.'

While he shifted across to the driving seat, she slipped out, stuffed blanket and tarpaulin between mud and wheel then stood back.

'Okay,' she called.

'Push!' he shouted back.

She braced a foot against the stone gatepost behind her and placed both hands squarely on the van's rear. She felt rust beneath her fingers and imagined her fists bursting straight through bodywork that was little more than filler and cheerful paint.

'Okay,' she called again.

He revved. The wheels churned uselessly, burying the blanket and chewing up the tarpaulin.

'Stop,' she called. 'Stop! I can feel her sinking.'

All about them glossy four-wheel-drives were pulling away. She thought of asking for help but she knew what the swinging headlamps revealed; an ageing New Age couple and an even older van. She imagined women taking in the mud caked round her inappropriate shoes and sprayed up her faded Indian cotton, heard their hastily mouthed commands to their husbands to pay no heed and hurry on by. She knew she and Corey presented the very image of fecklessness, of thankless time-wasting.

Corey was losing his temper. He had a child's inability to deal with stress and so had designed his life along lines of dull simplicity. His back-to-basics philosophy masked a fear of confrontation and un-expected challenges. He had made a big effort, she knew, coming out tonight, sitting restlessly through a concert of what he called *her* music but the effort was worthless for being so paraded. An evening of his reluctantly given was small recompense for the tedious hours she had spent driving him back and forth from the lay-by where he peddled the crude wooden mushrooms he 'carved' with a chainsaw. Even so, he was going to make her pay.

'Why'd you stop pushing?' he asked.

'I told you,' she said. 'It's sinking. You'll only make it worse.'

'This was a stupid idea, parking in here.'

'There was nowhere else to park.'

'You knew we'd get stuck. If those chickens are dead . . .'

'I'll buy you some new ones.'

'Oh yes. Money solves everything. Wave your wand and spend your father's precious money.'

'Excuse me?' Gretel turned her back to flag down the last four-wheel-drive as it began to pull out. Grinning, actually grinning, the driver wound down his window.

'Sorry,' he said. 'Daren't stop or we'll get stuck too.'

'Good luck,' the woman beside him called and they purred away.

As Gretel stood aside to let them pass, the mud sucked off one of her inappropriate shoes. She groped in the dark for it but her fingers found only ooze and she nearly lost her balance.

'Oh. God, I'm so sorry.'

It was the young man in the dinner jacket who had waved them in. She had spotted him later, in the chorus, cheeks pink with effort, eyes shining with emotion. His white shirtfront glowed bluish in the light of the moon. He shone a torch across them then politely dropped its beam.

'Can I help push?'

169

'Better not,' she said. 'We might sink even further.'

'I should never have let you park here. Come on. I'll shove too.'

So they pushed again while Corey revved again and the van sank up to its rear axle. Uncomplaining, the young man now wore mud on his shirtfront like a penance.

'I could ring the AA or something,' he suggested, shining a torch into the liquefied mire.

'We're not members,' she said and it felt as though she were confessing to not being members of society. 'I normally fix the van myself.'

'Oh. Well, I'd offer to pull you out myself but I've only got a 2CV. Erm. Tell you what, the chairwoman's got a Land Rover.'

'Oh goodie,' Corey said, mimicking his accent. 'And where's she?'

'She'll be up at the pub, I expect. I'll drive up there now and see if I can find her. If I do, I'll send her right back with a tow-rope. Or I'll send someone else. It won't be more than half an hour max.'

'Oh brill,' Corey said and swore.

'I feel awful about this,' the young man went on. 'You'll never want to come again.'

'No no,' Gretel said.

'Quite right,' said Corey.

'There'll be two free seats for you on the last night. I'll have them left on the door for you. I'm sorry there's not much more I can do.'

'It's not your fault. Honestly,' she said. 'Thanks for everything.'

He found her missing shoe before he left and handed it over with further apologies then he disappeared into the lane. Moments later they heard his 2CV gunning uncertainly and pulling away. There was no one left besides them. The night enveloped them, as did Corey's filthy mood.

Gretel tried turning on the radio to lighten the atmosphere but he told her not to waste the battery. She said she wished she'd known to bring a picnic like everyone else, then they might have had leftover sandwiches to enjoy. Which of course made things worse because now he was hungry as well as stranded.

Suddenly he was getting out.

'Where are you going?' she asked.

'Home,' he said.

'But he said it would only be half an hour.'

'So? They could all be dead by now. Anyway, what makes you think he was telling the truth? He'll be in the pub with his mates. He'll be drinking. No one'll come. I'm off.'

'But how . . .?'

'I'll hitch,' he said. 'Your van. Your mess. You wait.'

'Don't go,' she said. 'Don't be like that. This is silly. You'll never find a lift.'

But he did, almost immediately. A Beetle stopped,

a new one, and when the light came on inside she saw the young woman driving it, blonde, sporty-looking, a surfing type. She heard him say, quite distinctly as he got in, 'Oh, she'll be all right,' and he sped away without a backward glance.

Alone at last, unhurried and with no headlamps to spoil the clarity, she found herself in the perfect situation to admire the comet. It was the first she had seen. Until now she had always assumed they were swift blazes in the night sky, like shooting stars. Or perhaps shooting stars were simply other planets' comets? Her grasp of astronomy was vague but she had always wondered how the superstitious, the Three Wise Men, the invaded Saxons on the Bayeux Tapestry, could have built such significance on something one might blink and miss. Instead, she now saw, comets were like frozen things, speeding, maybe, but at such a distance they barely seemed to move.

She'll be all right. She repeated his words in her head like a mantra. The Brahms had stirred her up, brought her repeatedly close to tears with its grand talk of death, of mourning, of last things and grass-like flesh. It left her exposed and childlike, in need of the kind of hugs Corey only offered when drunk and unhelpfully sentimental but the comet at once belittled and calmed her. *Nothing matters*, it said and *Everything is possible*.

Gretel removed her second shoe, so as not to lose

it, then walked barefoot to the back of the van. The squelching mattered less without shoes on. It was only mud. It would wash off. She turned on the light and closed the door behind her. There was water in the flask and gas in the canister. She set the kettle on to boil. There were some Garibaldi biscuits in the tin beside the teabag jar, softened with age but still quite palatable. Munching while she waited for her tea, she checked the cupboards. The tools were there, naturally, and the jack – one drove a van this old nowhere without them – but so were the van's original picnic set, the road atlas, her duffel coat and a good thick jersey she had given up for lost. The mud would not have done anything to the blanket a launderette could not undo. Her wallet was empty of notes but it held the card only she could use, *the Card of Power* as she thought of it. Her driving licence, stowed behind the sun visor, seemed suddenly the official recognition of some much deeper ability than mere self-transport. She dunked her teabag and made a mental list of all she would be leaving behind if she failed to follow Corey. A heap of old clothes, old paperbacks, her clumsy attempts at pottery and an attractive, straggle-haired hitch-hiker she had once rescued from a downpour on Salisbury Plain. Nothing she could not replace, should the need arise.

The festival chairwoman arrived with Land Rover, tow-rope and a tactful lack of expressed surprise at finding one person where she had been led to expect two. She pulled the van back out to tarmac then paused, after unhitching the rope which, miraculously, had not pulled off its bumper. Her manner was bracing in a good, old-fashioned way that instilled confidence rather than terror.

'Are you positive you'll be all right?' she asked as though on the verge of offering a warming mustard bath and a serviceable change of clothes.

Gretel felt the mud crack on her cheek so she must have been smiling.

'I'll be fine,' she said. 'Honestly.'

THE EXCURSION

The idea was to make a full day of it rather than have the demonstration as the be-all and end-all. The minibus collected them from outside the church at ten-thirty. Gwen and Bernie bagged three seats at the back so she could sit with them.

They were like that, Eileen had realized. Forceful.

People who escaped from inside aeroplanes seconds before they turned to fireballs did so because for a few moments something in their genetic make-up enabled them to override all inculcated sense of decency to trample on the hands and faces of other passengers in a single-minded rush for life. Afterwards they would say how guilty they felt and people assumed this reflected a becoming sense of un-worthiness at being spared. Actually what they spoke of was uncomplicated guilt at their memories of elbowing an air steward in the face or punching a dithering child aside from the escape chute.

Gwen and Bernie were such people and Eileen was not. They bagged her a seat because they wanted her with them but if the minibus were balanced on a cliff, they'd jump out without a backward glance at her.

They were big-boned, wet-lipped, hot-palmed meat-eaters; more like brother and sister than husband and wife. She preferred not to imagine them naked.

It was not far. A forty-minute run on the motorway then half that again dawdling in queues through the city's outskirts and system of roundabouts. Someone had a daughter-in-law in the police who had tipped them off so they knew exactly where to meet up and when. There were two hours to kill so they tried on shoes in Marks – Gwen was a martyr to corns, apparently – before enjoying a sort of package-deal OAP lunch in the café at the top of Dingles.

She had not known them long. They had met through church. Eileen had attended the same church most of her life. She believed in Father and Son and – if not pressed for specifics – Holy Ghost. She accepted the probable truth of much of the Bible and found a recital of the Lord's Prayer a great comfort at times of stress. She disengaged her intellect when joining in the Creed but she would unhesitatingly have ticked any box marked Christian.

She worshipped at the church her mother had preferred, which embraced an undemonstrative, tasteful brand of Anglicanism, a church for women like herself who were happy enough to lend a hand at a fundraising bazaar but preferred their religion undiscussed and uninvolving.

At least she thought that was the sort of woman she was. Then Gwen and Bernie turned up in the congregation one Sunday – the numbers were never spectacular so one could always spot new faces – and sat beside her. It was one of the few churches in the diocese that persisted in holding out against doing the Peace but they startled her by clasping her hands in theirs at the moment in the service where other priests might have intoned *let us offer one another a sign of peace* and murmuring, 'Peace be with you,' with such urgency she spent the rest of the service worried that hers was not so tranquil a soul as she had thought.

They sought her out during coffee and biscuits afterwards and introduced themselves.

'We can tell you're not happy here,' Gwen said. 'Can't we, Bernie? I mean, it's not right. Not right for you. I'm sure he's a lovely man but you have to go back to first principles, sometimes.'

'I'm sorry?' Eileen said, confused.

By way of explanation, Bernie nodded towards Reverend Girouard, who had not long been with them. '*Homosexual,*' he hissed.

179

'Shame,' said Gwen. 'It's a lovely church other-wise. Old.'

'He even wants to bless their unions,' Bernie added. 'He asked the bishop.'

Eileen had already gathered from the flower arrangers that there was no likelihood of a Mrs Girouard and that Mr Clancy, who had been giving organ recitals for a while now, was possibly rather more than a lodger at the vicarage. The two men were exceptionally polite and good-looking and, after her initial surprise, she had begun to decide that their domestic arrangement made a pleasant change from the previous incumbent who had one of those resentful, difficult wives who seemed almost standard C of E issue these days and played Divide and Rule with the ladies on the flower rota. She had not analysed her response very deeply but a small part of her pleasure stemmed from the sense that she was not reacting as her parents would have done. Her unvoiced welcome of the two men was a timid rebellion against the norm. Now she found she lacked the courage to give it voice, however, and felt shamed into agreeing with Gwen and Bernie.

'I know,' she heard herself sigh. 'It probably isn't right. I mean, not ideal. But what can one do? We're lucky to have a priest at all, as far as I can see.'

'One that's white, you mean,' sighed Bernie.

'That's not what I . . .' Eileen began.

'Vote with your feet,' Gwen cut in. 'Next week you're coming to us at St Mungo's.'

She could have laid low, perhaps, pleaded sickness or lain out of sight on the kitchen floor when Gwen came tapping on the window with her wedding ring. She had gone with them, however, meek as a lamb.

St Mungo's was not at all the sort of church her mother would have liked, so initially there was a tacit satisfaction in changing allegiances. The hymns were happy and unfamiliar, their words projected onto a big screen so that everyone's hands were left unencumbered for waving in the air or clapping. The priest was a muscular, short-haired man – like a soldier or PE instructor – who wore a plain suit instead of robes and kept walking among them and making eye contact so that everything in the service felt tremendously personal. The Peace was no mere embarrassed handshake but a heartfelt festival of greeting in which people actually left their pews to meet strangers across the aisle. The priest tracked her down. There was no escaping him. Offset by his short silver hair, his eyes were chips of sapphire.

'I'm Paul,' he said, offering a hand both large and warm.

'Eileen,' she told him. 'I'm Eileen Roberts.'

'Peace be with you, Eileen,' he said, bringing his other hand into play so that both of hers were trapped. 'Welcome to St Mungo's. I mean that. Truly.'

And she felt so hot behind her eyes she thought she might faint.

His handshake was so firm and his welcome so compelling that she proved unswervingly disloyal and came back to St Mungo's week after week. Reverend Girouard was undoubtedly better bred but there was no denying that his twinkly charm was effete by comparison, weak even, and she reminded herself – and her mother's disapproving shade – that some of the disciples had been rough-edged working men, men her father would have dismissed as *common*.

Gwen and Bernie did not come every week. She soon realized this was because they worked as covert missionaries, targeting churches where the priests were unmarried or unorthodox, to lure away to St Mungo's discontented worshippers who might otherwise have left the church entirely.

'I suppose it's all the same God, though,' Eileen let slip in a weak moment and Bernie corrected her.

'Yes, but some vessels are unworthy, Eileen. You wouldn't serve your guest on unclean china.'

She had since seen Reverend Girouard's good-looking friend Mr Clancy on the High Street a couple of times and crossed the street quickly to avoid any awkwardness. Reverend Girouard himself had come round once and actually called her name through the letterbox when she failed to answer the bell. She hid from him in the broom cupboard in case he peered through a window and saw her. She felt ill afterwards from the excitement and had to lie down.

There was already a small crowd outside the law courts but, tipped off by the policewoman daughter-in-law, they knew to stand in a less obvious position down a side street where the authorities thought the van could emerge unimpeded.

They had all enjoyed a glass of wine with lunch and, as they waited, Gwen expounded on the accused's crimes with something approaching relish. Eileen did not take a newspaper as a rule because the photographs upset and haunted her. She preferred the radio, whose rare horrors one could always switch off. But Gwen talked horrors now, how the victims had been young men, little more than boys really, how they had been drugged and sexually preyed upon, how there were signs for those who knew how to read them that his purposes had been Satanic. He had shown no remorse and had even laughed to himself as the judge read out the charges.

What they told her fired her up with disgusted indignation but still she was not the sort of woman to make a spectacle of herself in public. As the time grew ever nearer she became increasingly tense, not wanting to be singled out for holding back, but not wanting either to behave in a way that was extreme. But just as the gate was swinging open and the unmarked van emerging, Gwen thrust a box of eggs into her hand from the collection she had picked up cheaply in Poundstretcher.

'He laughed to himself as the judge read out the charges,' she said. 'Just think of that. He laughed, Eileen!'

The crowd surged out into the road and Eileen was swept along with it. She knew she'd have to join in, she knew she'd have to throw an egg at least if only to do what was expected of her. But as the van drew near and the people around her started to shout, 'Filth! Filth!', and to throw things she shouted the first thing that came into her head.

'Satan!' she shouted. 'Murdering Satan!'

A sort of heat rose up behind her eyes, as rapidly as boiling-over milk, and her head was suddenly full of the poor boys, of lads she had known who might have been the killer's victims.

The rear of the van was blanked out, of course, and she found she directed all her uprush of hate at the startled man who was driving, not quite hidden by the grilles over the van's windows. She fancied there was fear in the look he gave her before the police came to his rescue and made the crowd stand back to let him pass.

It was over in seconds. She felt her cheeks on fire and found she was laughing, almost hysterical with embarrassment, by the time the van was rounding the corner. Bernie looked at her with respect.

'It's the Spirit,' he said. 'The Spirit is on you!'

But it wasn't, she knew. Gwen knew it too, glancing at her with a woman's sharper instinct. Eileen had tasted something more like ecstasy and her flesh was alight in a way that made her want to hide herself. She was disgusted with herself too. She had only meant to join in a little. It was quite unlike her to be so carried away and hatred was an emotion of which she had little experience.

On the minibus home everyone was chattering and excited, as though they had been abseiling or done a bungee jump at an age when no one would have expected it of them. Eileen pretended to join in but she was thoughtful, disturbed at the emotional roiling their messy little demonstration had set off in her.

By the time they were being dropped outside the church again, her old mute passivity had fallen on her however and she was easily persuaded back to Gwen and Bernie's for a restorative cup of tea.

It was an unremarkable house, over-furnished with unremarkable things; a house in a gravy advertisement. She donated a box of fondant fancies she had bought in Marks and was saving for later. Gwen sliced up a Battenberg and passed it round. The pieces were far bigger than Eileen would have allowed herself. She normally made a Battenberg feed eight, not three. She broke her slice into more manageable blocks of sponge and icing.

'Hey,' Gwen said. 'Show Eileen the tape.'

'Are you sure?' Bernie asked.

'Oh, she's one of us, now,' Gwen said, dabbing a pink crumb from the corner of her lips. 'Aren't you, Eileen?' She had not finished her mouthful properly. Eileen saw mashed cake on her tongue. 'After this afternoon's display,' Gwen chuckled. 'Eh, Eileen, who'd have thought you had it in you!'

So Eileen sat on in a vast Parker Knoll recliner like an imprisoning dentist's chair – Bernie had yanked up the footrest because they knew she had vein trouble – and watched a video with them.

It was a home-made affair, crudely shot by their son who worked in the Middle East as an engineer with an oil company. Because of the crowds, the passing cars, the glimpses of women, children, people on mobile phones, it took her a while to decipher what she was supposed to be focusing on. Then she saw the diminutive figures beyond the bustling fore-ground, figures in a clearing of bloodstained sand. It was, she understood as Gwen began her fascinated commentary, footage of punishments and executions, shot by the son with a hidden camera. It was not all shot on the same occasion or even in the same place. He was an ever-ready collector, like a trainspotter; a connoisseur of extreme justice.

She glanced away from the screen long enough to take in again the photograph on the mantelpiece her eyes had skated over earlier in a restless search for something beautiful. There he was. A mixture of Gwen and Bernie. Big-boned. Cheerful. Smirking in his mortarboard. Her eyes were drawn back to the screen.

There were floggings for adultery and lechery and removal of hands for theft. There were stonings and, astonishingly, beheadings. The shootings were shockingly banal by comparison, because they were so familiar from films yet quieter and less dramatic than anything faked. (Gwen and Bernie afforded these their slightest respect and talked across them, ordinary talk about food plans, neighbours, fish-food pellets.) Then there was a scene so specific yet so odd that she could not quite believe what she was seeing and, reading her mind, Bernie rewound the tape to show her again.

Two men were pushed to their knees then tied to a stake. Then everyone backed away to allow a bulldozer to cause a sizeable wall to topple onto them, hiding them from view in dust and rubble. There was a cheer from the crowd on the video and an answering murmur of assent from Bernie.

'Homosexuals,' Gwen said. 'They used to stone them apparently until someone decided that was spiritually unclean for the executioners.'

'Splashes,' Bernie explained.

'So they topple a wall,' Gwen said. 'Go on, Bernie. Show her again.'

Somehow Eileen found the lever to lower the footrest and made it out of the chair and onto her feet. Somehow she found excuses and even thanks to stammer before finding her way out without actually seeming to flee.

Back at her house she locked the front door behind her, ran to the bathroom and brought up everything, OAP lunch, fondant fancies, Battenberg. She rid herself of everything of the afternoon but the stains in her memory, the fear in the driver's eyes, the admiration of ingenuity in Gwen's voice. She heard the woman's placid suburban tone, that would have been no different if she had been explaining a cunning technique for building a rockery or installing a water feature.

The spasms were so violent she had to wrap her arms about the lavatory bowl, and left her so weak that she rested her cheek against its cold porcelain for minutes afterwards, still hearing Gwen and seeing atrocities.

'We missed you,' Reverend Girouard said as he shook her hand after the next Sunday's service. His grasp was so coolly reassuring she found herself imagining how it might feel to hold his hand across her face. 'Daniel – Mr Clancy – thought you might have forsaken us for St Mungo's.'

Mr Clancy passed them, dunking a custard cream in his coffee. 'The dark side,' he murmured flirtatiously.

'I tried it out,' she admitted. 'Because they asked and it seemed rude not to. But it wasn't for me. They do the Peace, you know and it's all a bit much.'

'Well, welcome back,' he said and Eileen saw how it was possible to feel at once judged and forgiven by a smile.

HUSHÈD CASKET

They found it quite by chance. There was nothing on the map or in the guidebooks. Sons of hysterical women addicted to spontaneity, they were both methodical men, keen and meticulous planners. They had spent half the morning at Beverley Minster and had calculated on squeezing in the churches at Patrington and Hedon before they stopped for a late, wintry picnic. An unscheduled diversion was no more in character than trusting in fate to provide a palatable provincial lunch.

Hugo nearly didn't stop. He was a fast but inhibited driver and hated ever having to swerve onto a verge or lay-by to execute a three-point turn.

'Stop!' Chris told him, flapping a hand against Hugo's forearm. 'Please. Something really interesting . . .' And he made Hugo pull over and park so they could walk back, armed as ever with camera and sketch pad. 'Through here!' he called, hurrying ahead.

They had entered what passed for a valley in Yorkshire's seaward south-east. There was a press of overgrown trees beside the lane. What might once have been a lych gate had been smothered in ivy and neglect and all but lost beneath bird-sown elder and holly.

'There's nothing there,' Hugo insisted, glancing between the map and photocopies he had taken of the relevant pages of *England's 1000 Best Churches*. 'Probably just a barn or . . .'

But Chris pressed on, ducking under the holly. He had glimpsed a buttress as they flew past and was anticipating a little Gothic Revival jewel or at least one of those architectural riddles that made church-crawling such an addictive pleasure. The guidebooks had missed things before. Only two days into their honeymoon they had found a magnificent Saxon font, which alone was worth three stars, in an unlisted church they had only visited to track down the key-holder for one that was in all the books. Besides, he was the pretty one in the partnership, used to a fairly generous wilfulness allowance.

There was little left of the original building – a foreshortened nave, badly patched up with some decidedly agricultural breeze-block masonry. The old chancel and apse had been left to collapse, cut off by a new east wall and a crude, inappropriate window. What might once have been an avenue of clipped yew from lych gate to porch now formed a forbidding canopy, chilling the sunless air beneath it. But it was still a church where the map marked nothing, so Chris waited in the porch in triumph for Hugo to catch up.

'Well spotted,' Hugo said, picking a yew berry off Chris's shoulder, and Chris felt a flush of pathetic pride. The significance of his having at last found a lover whose preferred bedtime treats were lives of the likes of Ninian Comper or monographs on East Anglian corbels and whose top ten was not of dance tracks but bell towers passed him by in his happiness at having finally found the right match. It was his mother, waving them off on this eccentrically unsensuous honeymoon, who slyly observed that he had married his father. And she should know. Hugo wasn't conventionally sexy or notably rich so perhaps his main attraction for Chris were these small, heart-bumping instances – when he correctly dated a clerestory or found them some five-star Norman in a deeply unpromising suburb – of fatherly approval.

The porch displayed none of the usual vital signs of even remote parish business: no flower rota, no service list, no contact number for longsuffering key-holders, not even a notice about closing the door behind one so as to stop birds becoming trapped. There was no noticeboard, even, just plaster-work mapped with bright patches of green. Another curiosity was that the door was fastened from the outside, with two stout bolts so rusted and unused that Hugo had to take off a boot and wallop them with its heel to persuade them to shift.

By rights the hinges should have let out an echoing whine and skeins of cobweb sprung down from around the lintel. Such touches of Gothic might have offered camp comfort. Instead the door opened soundlessly onto a space where one felt not even a spider would have lived for long. There were no pews, or pulpit, no altar even. There was only a tomb, grey with dust, a large cardboard box and a font. There were none of the usual accretions a church gathered about itself with age – no memor-ials to virtuous wives or to sons lost in cruelly distant colonies, no antiquated cast-iron radiators, no mildewed hymnbooks, no stoutly tapestried kneelers and no electricity. Were it not for the font, it would hardly have seemed like a church at all. The interior had been scraped and replastered in the late 1800s, to judge from the tell-tale use of treacly wood stain on the undistinguished roof timbers. The windows – nonrepresentational stained glass, a fiery red margin around that peculiarly gloomy Victorian green – must have been replaced at around the same date, possibly following whichever fire or disaster had wrecked the original east end and left the place so stripped and truncated.

'Hardly feels like a church at all,' Chris said then wished he hadn't because the words gave the place permission to feel sinister. Hugo only let out a pre-occupied *huh* for answer. He was already busy photographing. That was what they did usually: he photographed the whole while Chris executed quick watercolours or sketches of telling details, gargoyles, carvings and so on, the two elements to be combined eventually in an album.

By their usual standards the building was not even second rate, but the tomb and font were arresting. The tomb was ancient. Whatever inscription it had borne had long since worn away but it was of a type with one they had seen in St Martin's, Lowthorpe, where the sculptor had demonstrated considerable bravura in portraying the corpse as so many mounds and dips beneath a shroud. The Lowthorpe monument was of a married couple, however, its shrouded bier a grim parody of a wedding bed. This showed just one body, a man's, uncomforted by pomp at its head or pets at its feet. It had been defaced, an angry cavity chipped away where the genitals had perhaps been too generously suggested for later sensibilities.

Chris sketched rapidly, his mind half on the need to press on if they were to do justice to Patrington

195

before dusk. He used charcoal, as it was apt for conveying the sweeps and shadows of carved cloth. Hurrying on to choose the best angle from which to sketch the font in pencil, he felt again the sense of dread that had pricked him when he dared to imagine the place was *not quite a church*. The font was carved from a basalt so black and so smoothed with age it might have been lead. It could have been pre-Christian, of course, and simply adopted for baptismal rites; he had seen such things before. It had figures on it, crudely carved, which appeared to be engaged in a dance or procession around its base, led by a taller figure dancing backwards with arms outstretched.

He jumped at the sound of the door thumping closed and glanced round to find he was alone. Hugo would be circling the outside, hunting for clues to the age the interior's shoddy restoration had masked. One of the crucial differences in their approaches to church-crawling was that whereas Chris required something attractive or at least amusing to hold his attention, Hugo could become entranced by a dull piece of lead detailing or some sidelined and anonymous lump of wood he was convinced might once have been a Golgotha.

Chris had glanced at his watch, shut his pad and been all set to follow him when his eye was drawn to the cardboard box. Had the church, or whatever the building now was, been even half as cluttered as they usually were, his gaze would have slid straight over it. The lack of clutter, however, the absence of the usual flower-arranging junk, stall of unloved books or garishly inappropriate Sunday school art projects, lent it a peculiar resonance. As did its placing. For, quite accidentally of course, it had been left on the floor at just the point where one would have expected to find an altar.

Hearing Hugo's whistling, he snapped charcoal and pencils back into his cunningly adapted spectacles case and made for the door . . . then stopped with the chilled handle under his fingers. There was no one here to laugh at him so he darted back to indulge his instincts and tidy the box off to one side where it wouldn't be the first thing visitors saw on entering. The place was depressing enough without litter.

The cardboard was damp, almost soaked through. He'd picked it up firmly and his grasp was enough to make it give way. Something fell onto his shoes. He tossed aside the cardboard, revolted, and looked down. It was a battered nylon sports bag of the sort carried by youths selling poor quality tea towels and nail brushes door-to-door. Or by burglars.

He crouched down to unzip it, half-expecting a cache of silver candlesticks and picture frames. The light in the building was so dim and the bag so dark that at first he thought it must be empty, then his questing hand found wood.

It was a tea caddy. George II, he'd have said, of an elegant sarcophagus design with little ball feet. Damp had left the wood blue with mildew, which made him sneeze. It was hard to judge its condition on the spot but he felt at once the unquestioning urge to acquire that often possessed him in junk shops and auction houses. He could tell at once how good it would look lovingly restored to its former lustre, with the other bibelots on the half-moon table behind his study sofa. He wanted it. He had to have it. Leaving it behind to moulder still further would be an act of cruelty and that was that.

Hugo coughed impatiently. Chris zipped the caddy back in the repellent bag, virtuously scrumpled up the mass of sodden card along with it for safe disposal in a proper place and hurried out to him.

Hugo was predictably horrified. 'You can't just *take* it!'

'Someone else did. It was obviously stashed here by some kid who nicked it and then didn't know what to do with it,' he suggested. 'Got shot of the iPods and jewellery then panicked and dumped it. It's nothing to do with the church. If it *is* a church still. I mean, it's an abandoned building, for Christ's sake. Look at it!'

As a sop to both their consciences, he wrote a quick note on a pad from the car and pinned it to the door. *Found here: antique wooden tea caddy.* By an instinct born of long years of bad dating, he made one of the zeroes in his mobile number look deliberately like a six. The note was fluttering in the wind as he left it; he had every hope it would not last the night.

The base Hugo had rented from the Landmark Trust for their honeymoon grandly described itself as a castle. It was actually just the surviving gatehouse and banqueting chamber of a medieval bishop's country residence, still fantastically atmospheric for all that it was only a fragment. Both main rooms were magnificently vaulted. There was a tremendous spiral staircase to a roof terrace with unnervingly low crenellations around its edge. Even the bathroom had an oriel window.

While Hugo fricasséed chicken and sang along to a Barbara Cook CD, Chris found dusters and beeswax furniture cream in the housekeeping cupboard and set to work on the caddy. It was every bit as good as his instincts had told him. The condition was perfect. It was made of mahogany or rosewood – or something more exotic as it was oddly weighty – and there was a lozenge of ivory inlaid about the keyhole. His determination to keep it grew as he made the wood shine once more. By the time Hugo was calling him to the supper table he had made up his mind that if anyone did ring up about it, he would pretend they had a wrong number, even if Hugo was in the room.

Hugo could be shamingly honest. It was one of

the things Chris cherished about him, along with his not smoking. When obliged now to put the correct money for postcards into a church's honesty box instead of the usual deceptively clattering collection of coppers, he would soothe his irritation by telling himself, *I married a Man of Principle*. He thought of it like that, with capitals, like the title of an Edwardian novel.

But perhaps the principles were weakening. As Chris set the caddy down without comment on the candlelit dining table, Hugo murmured, 'Oh. That *is* nice, isn't it? I expect you were right. Someone stole it then lost interest when they couldn't get it open. Either that or they didn't like to try selling it without a key. Odd, though, that they didn't try to force the lock. Hope this is okay. I forgot tarragon vinegar so it might be a bit rich with all this cream.'

It hadn't even occurred to Chris that the caddy was locked until Hugo mentioned it. Now it irritated him throughout supper. Beneath their roving conversation, his mind kept returning to the subject like a tongue to a chipped tooth.

There was no television or radio to lull them into somnolence and the small fire had little effect on the warmth of so vast a room, so they retired far earlier than usual. Chris read an M.R. James ghost story and Hugo, who had no patience with fiction, read James's essay on the Lady Chapel sculptures at Ely. Then they made clumsily perfunctory love, possibly because they were both so wide awake, which sort of petered out. Rather than slip into blissful oblivion, they lay there fidgeting for a while then Hugo apologetically turned his bedside lamp back on and returned to his abbeys while Chris, thus released, slipped back downstairs on the muttered pretext of thirst.

He ransacked the chest of drawers where games and jigsaws and the accumulated detritus of many holidays were stashed. It was even colder down-stairs now that the fire had gone out and his dressing gown was only of silk. He was shivering and on the verge of giving up when he found what he needed: a couple of grimy paperclips adrift in a leaking Monopoly box.

One of his earlier, less judiciously chosen lovers had taught him how to give better blowjobs, how to break into a car with a wire coat hanger and how to use two partially uncoiled paperclips to pick small scale Georgian and Victorian warded locks.

He worked on the caddy at the dining table. It took him longer than usual because his hands were sweating with nerves for some reason, and he had to break off repeatedly to wipe them so as not to lose his grip on the wires.

The lock gave suddenly, startling him. The hinge turned on an unusually powerful concealed spring, which caused the lid to fly open with a bang as soon as the little lock's levers gave under pressure. There must have been a gust of wind down the chimney or up the stair at the same moment for a kind of shudder passed through the building, fluttering curtains and causing two of the doors to slam.

Chris held the caddy to the light and was surprised to find it quite bare inside; in the second that it opened, he thought he had caught a glimpse of something like ash inside it. He saw it was lined, most atypically, with lead, hence his having thought the wood so unusually dense. It couldn't have been for tea after all. A tiny sarcophagus for a small pet, perhaps? A tamed starling or tiny marmoset whose mourning owner wanted them kept beside her but not so close as to have body fluids leaking through the joinery onto her writing desk.

But the need for a spring was a mystery. He tried pressing the lid closed again and found there was no catch to keep it shut so it flew wide again immediately. By instinct, he raised the casket to his face and sniffed its insides. There was none of the normal antique smell – no ghost of bergamot or lavender dust. There was only the unmistakably frank musk of warm, male groin. It cut through the honeyed overlay of the polish he'd applied earlier like a dirty laugh in a silent order.

Shocked, amused and, for all the chill and their recent fumblings, turned on, Chris pressed his nose in deeper to breathe it in again then flicked out the light and hurried back upstairs to show Hugo.

'I got it open at last,' he called up as he rounded the stair's spiral. 'And I think I can see why someone locked it, because of these sprung hinges. But get a whiff of—'

He was startled to find Hugo not curled up half-asleep with M.R. James but standing naked in the doorway, waiting for him. Usually fairly slow to get started, he already had a pornographic hard-on and his eyes were glittering like splintered coal.

'On your knees, Boy,' he said in a voice he had never used before. 'And worship.' He snatched the casket and tossed it aside then pushed Chris roughly down to the icy stone threshold.

As was explained earlier, their recently registered partnership was founded on the principle that Chris was the pretty, Hugo, the lucky one. The dynamic seemed to work for them both and Chris had never analysed it beyond noting occasional pangs for the craving he had felt with the picklock or some of the other Unpresentables.

Overnight it was as though their polarities had changed. In the days that followed, Hugo looked at him with nothing warmer than amusement and he found himself desiring without dignity or control. Hugo hadn't suddenly changed shape. His legs were still sturdy, still slightly out of proportion to his long trunk and wiry arms. He had not suddenly developed a rippling six-pack or a swimmer's shoulders but Chris had only to look at him to want to press his face into his belly or feel Hugo's forearm hairy against his lips. At a glimpse of Hugo's teeth or the way his hair grew in forks down the back of his (shortish) neck, something gave way within him and he felt no feeble sense of shame or decency could stop his wanting to possess or be possessed by him. Seeming to sense this, Hugo would give his newly characteristic smirk and murmur, 'Insatiable!' in a way that only made the hunger for abasement more intense.

As the holiday progressed, the casket went ignored, as did their stash of maps and guides and careful itineraries. Instead, Chris fell in with whatever whim seized Hugo – be it an afternoon lost to a seaside amusement arcade, an extravagant quest for new, frankly rather common clothes or an evening wasted on a terrible horror film full of lingering torture scenes – in the hope that his meekness or subservience, or whatever this was, would be rewarded by more sex and as soon as possible.

They had never been a couple that touched in public. Chris was perfectly happy, if not quite proud, to be gay but he disliked public displays of affection in anyone, had always thought them ill-mannered. Yet suddenly he was groping Hugo whenever he could, seizing his arse, his hand, his thigh – whatever Hugo would allow – immune to the angry or uncomfortable looks this provoked in others. Aside from a very few attempts in the first days of their courtship, they had only ever made love under cover of darkness. Now they were having sex in broad daylight, even in the open air, even in a corner of an otherwise unremarkable church.

It was in many ways the very thing one would hope for, but hardly dare expect, from a honeymoon, only it was so unlike who they were.

Chris made no connection between what was happening and the stolen casket until his phone rang on the fourth day.

Hugo had horrified him by going out on his own soon after breakfast, returning after two agonizing hours with a burly, donkey-jacketed road worker who was evidently as deeply under his spell as Chris. He had the road worker strenuously service them both in a kind of frenzy – hands and boots leaving tarry prints on the sheets – until the man seemed to come to his senses and announced in a broken undertone that his wife would be expecting him. Hugo had fallen into a deeply sated sleep so Chris pulled on a dressing gown and saw their visitor politely out.

The phone had gone unused for so long he had trouble tracking its ringing down to a pocket of the tweed coat he hadn't worn since Hugo called it *maidenly*, a few days before.

It was a woman. Fifty-something. Maybe younger,

but she sounded careworn. 'I found your note,' she said at once.

'Oh God,' Chris said. 'Is the caddy yours? I was so sure someone had stolen and dumped it and it was getting ruined by the damp. Where are you? I can jump in the car and bring it—'

She laughed, cutting him off. 'We don't want it *back*! I wish you all joy of it. Just tell me . . . have you *opened* it?'

'Well, I have to say I was a bit cheeky and I picked the lock with a couple of paperclips. The spring in the hinge was a bit of a surpr—'

There was a clatter.

'Hello?' he called out.

She had just dropped her phone on the nearest surface. Her voice grew rapidly fainter. She was calling to someone and laughing. Laughing almost wildly. 'Dee? Dee! He opened it! Oh my God! At last! Dee?' Her tone changed. 'Dee!' There was silence for a minute then footsteps coming closer and her rapid, asthmatic breathing. Then came the sound of three digits being dialled and then her voice again, frantic now. 'Bloody hell. Hang up, will you? I need to—'

Then it went dead as she succeeded in breaking the connection. Chris checked his phone's record of incoming calls but the display logged her simply as Unknown.

Shaken, feeling a little bruised after the morning's

unexpected extra exertions, he pulled his dressing gown more tightly about him and poured two tumblers of restorative Barolo – they had slipped into a holiday habit of daytime drinking – and bore them upstairs.

Their grandly vaulted bedroom reeked of sex in a way it had surely never done in the bishop's day. Hugo was still fast asleep, with just a sheet to cover him. His arms and legs were flung out in childlike abandon, as though sleep had caught him unawares. For all the room's iodine reek and the tarry finger-prints on his cheek and neck, he had an air of innocence about him. Chris set the wine on the bedside table as silently as he could and gently drew the blankets over the sheet to keep him warm. He realized he was looking down at him fondly, hungry for nothing but the quiet pleasure of gazing unchecked. He saw that he was thinking of Hugo's innocence as something *lost*.

As if by association, he glanced about them for the casket. For an instant he thought Hugo could have thrown it out in one of his new fits of temper, then he spotted it on its side beneath the chair where he had tossed his clothes earlier. It was still gaping open but when he picked it up he found its lid closed quite easily and stayed closed. Whatever had the woman been making such a fuss about? He set it on the dressing table, opening and shutting it a few times to see if there were some hidden catch he had missed. The spring must have broken when the casket fell to the floor. In the looking glass he saw Hugo stir, wake and stare at him from the mass of pillows.

'What are you up to?'

He whipped around guiltily. 'Playing with the box,' he said.

Then Hugo's eyes took on that glinting blackness again and Chris felt compelled to go to the bedside and offer him his glass of wine. If he looked even half as shattered as he felt, he must look half-dead, he thought. He longed for nothing and nobody but a long, inactive sleep followed, perhaps, by a gentle day of church-crawling across the Humber in northern Lincolnshire but, probed by Hugo's gaze, he found he was getting hard again.

'So. How did we compare?' Hugo asked. 'Was he man enough for you? Hmm?'

Chris tugged back the sheet to press one of Hugo's feet to his face and take its big toe deep into his mouth. He heard the unmistakable clack of the casket's lid flying open again.

There were only two days of honeymoon left. The ever-shrinking part of his mind that was still alert to things like time, diaries, responsibility and the need to return to his primary-school job the following week, struggled to form a plan and hold it in mental place long enough for its execution. A fox's yelping woke him in the depths of that night, while Hugo was still asleep, and he was able to slip across the room and close the box again. But when sunlight returned and Hugo had finished with him for the moment and gone to take a much-needed bath, he found the box open again and again as hard to close and keep closed, as if some unseen force were holding it wide. He knew he could only think or act freely when Hugo was asleep or out of the room. He hurried downstairs, past the mercifully closed bathroom door, found the bent paperclips in one of the plates Hugo had been using as an ashtray for his new cigar habit, and hid them in his dressing gown pocket. Then he hung the gown on the back of his bedroom chair and left the box close by it, oh so naturally positioned on the dressing table.

He knew minutes later he would neither know nor care about any of this but sensed, with a shred of survivor's instinct, that if he woke again in the night he would have exact comprehension of where they were and why. Having so plotted, it was with a mix of regret and sweet, quasi-suicidal abandon that he gave up halfway through the attempt to dress and went to tap on the bathroom door to ask if Master wanted his back scrubbed.

The day that followed was especially draining. Hugo fetched no more what he called *takeaways* but he insisted they drive all the way to a windswept funfair near Bridlington where he made Chris ride every sickening ride with him although he knew – or always *used* to know – that they brought on his labyrinthitis. And everywhere he flirted – with men, women and children alike. Everyone caught in that glinting stare responded like a dog to roasting chicken. Hugo seemed to feed off their eagerness to please, as if their quick devotion were a kind of fuel to him, but there was always a trace of mockery in his expression as they fawned on him.

'He despises us,' Chris thought, briefly freed by Hugo's taking a long, lascivious lick from a small boy's cheerfully proffered ice cream. 'He despises us for being merely human.' But then Hugo flicked his eyes back to him and smirked in a way that made Chris breathless with jealousy. He would have brained the child had its mother not arrived to snatch it away with a hot-cheeked apology.

After the possibilities of crude sensation had been exhausted in the funfair, Hugo made them gorge on seafood then he drove them at maniacal speed out to a car park near the bleak tip of Spurn Head where he pleasured a sequence of birdwatchers in their cars while Chris looked helplessly on through the misting car windows, half-wishing a policeman would intervene.

After such quantities of sea air and exercise and the wine Hugo encouraged him to drink over supper, they slept profoundly and it was not the fox yelping but an urgent need to piss that woke Chris shortly after dawn. Returning from the bathroom he saw Hugo's sleeping face, blameless and benign, and remembered the casket. He hurried over to it, all but slammed it shut then frantically worked the paperclips in its lock, his fingers cramped from tension in his hurry to work the mechanism before his clattering woke Hugo.

It locked and held fast. He tugged at the lid to test it then bundled the thing into a bag of dirty laundry that lay ready for their departure. He slipped back to the bed.

'Hugo? Hugs?' Hugo stirred at his touch and mumbled grouchily. The second he opened his eyes Chris could see he was himself again. They no longer looked coal-black but had resumed their old watery grey. They were even a little bloodshot. And his voice was his own once more: soft-edged, slightly peevish.

'What time is it?' he muttered.

'It's early. Sorry. I couldn't sleep. I thought I'd slip into town and bring back papers and croissants for our last breakfast. Before we start packing up, I mean.' He kissed him on the forehead. 'Go back to sleep.'

There was really no need to hide the casket but he left it in the laundry bag just to be safe and carried it down the winding stair with a heap of books, as though starting to load up the car.

He found a locksmith after driving around Selby's

one-way system a few times. He was clearly the first customer of the day. A small, sharp-featured woman in a nylon housecoat unbolted the door to let him in.

'He's in the back finishing his breakfast,' she said shyly. 'I'll send him out,' and she darted through a curtain at the back of the shop. Chris could smell toast and bacon. It felt curiously intimate, as if he were sharing their kitchen. The man, pinker, larger, brought his mug of tea out with him. He seemed friendlier than the wife, the sort of man who kept a lurcher and would murmur tendernesses to it when away from the house. Chris felt a pang of guilt and half thought to leave the box under his arm and make something up, buy a padlock instead. But then he saw himself in the mirrored back of a key ring display, saw how exhaustion had aged him by years in a matter of days, and he resumed his ruthless purpose.

'I need a key making for this,' he said. 'And the lock freeing up.'

The man took the box. 'Oh yes?' he said. 'Ooh. Heavy, ain't it?'

'Er. Yes. Don't shake it, though. It's . . . it's quite valuable.'

'Well that shouldn't be a problem. I can do it while you wait, if you like. I've a stash of old keys out back. One of them's bound to fit.'

The wife reappeared briefly, to cast an appraising

glance over the man's shoulder at the casket. She must have been listening in from the breakfast table.

'No hurry,' Chris stammered. 'Honestly. I've got a few other things to do in town. You finish your tea. I'll take one of your cards, if I may.'

'Right you are, then.'

As he left, the bell on the door jangled behind him in tinny accusation.

He drove off, bought a paper, found an old-fashioned baker's and bought them rolls for breakfast still warm from the oven and, from a shop nearby, local butter and honey. Instead of returning to the locksmith's, he drove back out towards Cawood and stopped by an ancient phone box on the edge of the village. He glanced at his watch. They'd surely had long enough. He took out the locksmith's cheap little card and rang the number on it.

The woman answered. A woman. Her voice was transformed and husky, somehow lubricated. 'Hello?'

'Oh. Yes. I brought the little tea caddy in for your husband about forty minutes ago. I wondered if he'd managed to get it open.'

'Oh yes,' she said. 'He got it open all right. Didn't you?' Her voice hardened suggestively. 'I said didn't you!'

Somebody mumbled something then cried out as if struck.

When she came back on the phone, her voice was so close he imagined he felt her breath, hot at his ear. 'That was very clever,' she purred. 'And rather nasty. Christopher.'

His hand shook so violently as he hung up that the receiver bounced off its bracket and swung with a clunk against the wall. He lurched out to the car and sped back to find Hugo.

The gatehouse was still quite silent. There were no signs of life from upstairs yet but neither was there that sense of all-seeing malignancy, he realized. They were free. They had been spared. He walked to the kitchen to put on the kettle and toss the rolls in the oven to keep warm. He poured an orange juice and downed it in three greedy draughts, its taste as fresh and clean as the reassertion of order. Then he filled a second glass and carried it upstairs.

Hugo didn't stir as he came in. He lay there with a hand thrown across his face as though to ward off a blow from an unseen assailant. It was such a pleasure to see him simply lie there, homely again, even vulnerable. Chris wouldn't wake him straight away.

DREAM LOVER

'What do you mean?' she said, fingers twined in his hair as he continued to nuzzle her awake. 'Of *course* you do. Everyone does.'

'Not me.'

'You must. If you didn't you'd . . .'

'Die?' He looked up from the breast to which he was paying sleepy homage. He grinned. 'I don't think so.'

'But everyone dreams. You must simply forget them.'

He shrugged. It could not have mattered less to him. She loved that in a man; that guileless, unquestioning confidence in his own normality.

'So how about you?' he asked. 'How'd you sleep?'

'Fine,' she said, thoughtfully.

'Did you . . .?'

'Well yes,' she said, remembering. 'I did. It was

217

rather amazing. You took me to a huge hotel and I was so excited but when they gave me the key to our room it was just a sort of drawer with a mattress in it. Not a room at all.'

'What happened then?'

'Well, I wasn't angry at all. It was rather cosy. You showed how you could lock me away and I'd be quite safe until you got back.'

'That turn you on?'

'Well yes. Yes it did. And then I . . . No. Don't stop. That's good.'

How could he not dream? Recalling and recounting her dreams was one of her earliest, deepest pleasures. The reality was probably scrappier, an impatient affair of hurried bowls of cereal and egg-stained school blouses, but when she recalled girlhood breakfasts, they came back as leisurely, sunlit affairs with her mother, all attention, asking her how she slept and whether she dreamed then listening, truly listening. If asked, she could date quite precisely the moment, aged nine, when she first understood the importance of escaping the family into marriage. The unpalatable insight came on the morning her baby sister first felt old enough to assert herself and interrupted the recounting of a dream with a weary sigh of, 'Boring!' The interruption was allowed to pass unrebuked by their mother. A terrible moment, that. A truly terrible one.

She had tried several men on for size until she found

this perfect fit. Healthy. Handsome. Good (e.g. not too extensive) fidelity record. Dead mother not overly mourned. Steady job. Own place. No unpresentable neuroses. An excellent lay. But now this. It was no more than a minor irritant. At first she actually liked the idea that he never dreamed but would listen intently while she recounted her night-narratives. It seemed all of a part with his uncomplicated maleness, like bristles or travelling light or having nothing in his bathroom cabinet but aspirin and a bottle of muscle rub. She began to boast of it in front of him.

'He doesn't *dream*!' she would exclaim. 'Isn't that so like a man?'

Friends would mock her, saying he must be keeping things from her, smutty fantasies, not-quite-forgotten girlfriends.

'Ask him,' she'd say and would delight in watching him shrug and tell them, 'What? So I don't dream. Is it a crime?' and she would cast him a proprietorial smile as he fended off her friends' inquisition.

She liked the difference between them because in many ways he was her superior – better paid, better educated, a lifetime non-smoker, a dumper not a victimized dumpee – but in this one sphere she could hold the upper hand. Compared to him, she entered sleep like a priestess into a tabernacle and emerged, her face shining with vision.

Then a business trip to Australia left her so badly jet-lagged that her sleep patterns were jangled for several days. She lay there beside him rejecting first one elbow then the other for sleeping on, holding him until she became unpleasantly hot, backing off from him until it seemed he was invading her space, even risking waking him by sitting up to read.

Waking him? Fat chance. He simply lay there, a secretive smile dimpling his stubbled cheeks, deep in self-sufficient slumbers. And not dreaming. And it began to disturb her that in sleep he could become such a blank, however pornographic; it reflected badly on her. Any fool could dream.

So why couldn't he?

There was a woman in the office called Magda, an older woman, who had been in therapy of one kind or another for so long she was something of an expert.

'I've got this friend,' she told Magda, 'who's desperate because she wants to keep a dream diary but she can't seem to remember her dreams long enough to write them down.'

The colleague smiled in a way that was not entirely friendly and shook her head with the worldly, self-satisfied air of one who has experienced everything and for whom life holds no more nasty surprises.

'I was just the same,' she said. 'We all are, tell her. You wake up and all these other thoughts start crowding in and the dream sort of crumbles. All she needs to do is write a little card saying any dreams question mark and stick it on her bedside table or her headboard or wherever she'll first look when she wakes up. If she does that and keeps a pad and pen handy too she'll soon find she stops forgetting. It'll become second nature. Did you want that last Cherry Bakewell or can I?'

So she tried it.

'Humour me,' she told him as she stuck a little, prettily lettered card to the edge of his bedside table.

'It won't work,' he said. 'I told you I don't dream. I never have.'

She hesitated a moment, tempted by simplicity, then remembered that his dreamlessness was a kind of insult because it meant he never dreamed of her.

'We'll see about that,' she said. 'Relax. Go to sleep. Forget the card's there.'

And at first nothing happened. For three mornings in a row they woke to the confidential murmur of the clock radio and he read the card that asked him any dreams question mark and answered nope and turned to her with an I told you so air.

On the fourth morning, however, although he still said nope he did so with a minute hesitation and he couldn't meet her eye afterwards.

'There *was* something!' she said, pouncing. 'Wasn't there?'

'No?'

'You dreamed. I could tell!'

'No.' He frowned. 'Well. Yes. Do you know, I think I may have done.' He laughed uneasily. 'But it sort of slipped away.'

'Never mind,' she said and kissed him, triumph warming her from within.

'I . . . I think it was a good one,' he said and frowned again. 'Damn.'

'Relax,' she said. 'Don't fret. Plenty more where that came from. Do you want your tea in bed this morning?'

They both drank heavily that night so their respective sleeps were a comatose blank, but the night after that he woke her up in his excitement.

'I dreamed,' he said.

'Wha—?' She was still half asleep.

'I dreamed. I really dreamed.'

'Great.' She sat up, rubbing sleep from her eyes. 'What happened?'

'I was in a field,' he began.

'Yes?' she prompted him at last. 'And?'

'That's it. I was in a field.'

'Is that all? What did you do there?'

'Nothing. Just stood, I suppose. But it was a big field, huge, and so green and the sky was this incredible blue. It was like one of those Renaissance paintings you like, like the background of a Piero. You know? How he sort of paints the silence?'

'Just you,' she repeated. 'In a field. Nothing else. No one else.'

222

'No. But I had this wonderful feeling. Something amazing was going to happen!'

'It was just a dream,' she said, indulging her need to flatten his spirits in her disappointment.

'Yeah,' he said, slumping beside her as he turned out the light. 'I guess.'

The next night they ate old French cheese which, cliché or no, had always produced spectacular results for her. Sure enough it seemed she had barely closed her eyes before she was living through an entire Barbara Stanwyck film, with her in the steamy lead role, fighting her way to the head office of a vast corporation by sleeping with a succession of ever more powerful and ugly, suited men. Only she didn't sleep with them because it was enough to know they wanted her and how badly. All she had to do was press them in the middle of the chest so their eyes narrowed with lust and she seemed fairly to light up with gratification. It was all superbly art directed, with restrained nineteen-forties details everywhere, flattering lighting, a great wardrobe and even tracking shots. And there was a magnificently bizarre climax in which she left the top of the building on a sort of flying desk, leaving all the pleading suits behind and below her.

But when the alarm woke them he was in there first, eyes bright with the need to relate a boyish extravaganza involving jungles, horses, treasure and a powerfully erotic encounter with the Foreign Secretary.

'But that's wonderful,' she managed. 'You dreamed. You really did this time.' She was about to cut in with her dream but found that somehow, in the effort of picturing his, she had lost all but a few greying rags of it.

'How about you?' he asked, touching her cheek with one finger in a way that had always faintly irritated her.

'What about me?'

'What did you dream about, Pumpkin?' He snuggled up to her which lessened the pain somewhat.

'Oh,' she said lightly. 'You know. Girl stuff.'

That night some rather pushy friends served them Cornish hen lobster for dinner. For her as for many, lobster was next only to mescalin and magic mushrooms in its ability to induce frightening dreams if eaten soon enough before sleep. She took off her make-up and climbed beneath the duvet with the same, not unpleasant queasy anticipation of a teenager taken to a slasher movie by a boy she wants to kiss.

Only the lobster affected him before it could take hold on her and she passed a shattering seven hours, repeatedly kicked or jolted awake as he became acquainted with his unconscious terrors. She returned to the office so grey-faced and lacking in concentration that two clients asked if she were unwell.

Making up the bed with fresh Egyptian cotton

that evening, she accidentally knocked the *any dreams?* card out of sight into the mess of out-of-favour shoes, old magazines and dust bunnies that lurked under the mattress. She did not retrieve it.

Now that there was no stopping him, however, he needed no encouragement. The dreams came thick and fast and, as he became adept at remembering them in ever-greater detail, he sometimes had as many as three a night to tell her, often beginning his urgent reports before it was even light. A lot of his dreams were about food, vehicles or thinly veiled desire for world domination. They rarely featured her and when she did appear it was never in a starring role but as a sort of cute younger sister (and she projected the cute part) gamely watching his exploits from a safe distance.

In the mornings, she began to slip out of bed before he woke sufficiently to start talking. She began to grow painfully tense between the shoulderblades if dinner-party conversation strayed from coffee offers to talk of sleeplessness. She began to take more notice of Brian from Accounts, a tantalizingly self-contained, rather handsome bachelor, who played squash every evening after work and had always struck her as an eminently sensible, feet-on-the-ground sort of man. Brian, she felt sure, was not a dreamer.

SLEEP TIGHT

The child's cry cut through the Schumann quintet Desmond was playing as he enjoyed a whisky after supper. He tried ignoring it at first and turned back to the article his brother had just published in a journal. *The Global Village,* he read, *Towards a Dialectic.* But the cry came again, more urgently, jangling his nerves and sending his glance skittering across the text. He swore under his breath, knowing he was being quite unreasonable, set down his book and glass and climbed the stairs.

'Coming,' he called out as cheerfully as he could.

The boy, Hamish, cried, 'Quickly! Please!'

'I'm here,' Desmond said, turning on the landing light and letting himself into the smaller spare room, his boyhood room, where he had thought to make the child at home among books and kites and ancient toy bears. 'Whatever is it? I thought to find you murdered after such a row.'

Hamish was sitting stiffly upright against the headboard, his eyes wet in the moonlight. 'It was the Moth Lady,' he said softly.

Desmond sighed, 'Her again,' and turned on the boy's bedside light, thinking it would comfort him.

'No!' Hamish cried out. 'No light! It makes her worse. It's the light that brings her.'

Desmond duly flicked off the light again, startled by the glimpse it had afforded of the boy's drawn, tear-stained face. 'Okay,' he said and sat on the edge of the bed. 'Hamish, I thought we'd discussed this. There's no Moth Lady.'

'But there *is*!'

'Well. There is in your dreams but in real life you're quite safe from her. There are moths because it's a warm summer night and they follow the lights and come in at the open windows. But there are none in here. They're all downstairs with me and my reading light.'

This rash stab at levity brought on another whimper.

'Look,' he said. 'I'll close your window. How's that? You'll still get fresh air from the open door. Better?'

There was a sniff and he could tell the child was nodding.

'Good boy. No more dreams now. Sleep tight.'

He returned, via a much needed top-up, to his

brother's supremely tedious article. His brother worked for a charity and was forever implying that this was a nobler pursuit than Desmond's picture restoration, although he earned three times as much. His salary had done little to leaven his prose style.

Desmond disliked children as a rule, his brother's in particular. He found them tedious and un-restrained. He associated them with noise, mess and primary-coloured plastic and regarded any friend embarked on parenthood as lost to a hostile power until further notice.

Hamish was an exception. Wary, thoughtful, bookish and apparently without friends, he reminded Desmond of himself in boyhood and it was a happy accident that he had acquired him, and not one of the more typical specimens, as a godson.

Hamish's unmarried mother, a curator and old friend, had often brought him to stay – cautiously at first, then with more confidence once she saw how he and Desmond warmed to one another, but this was his first visit on his own. She was away at a conference for two nights in the nearest univer-sity town and had dropped Hamish off en route.

'I shan't ring,' she said. 'It would only get him all churned up. But of course you can call me if there are any problems. There shouldn't be, though.'

For a seven-year-old he was, indeed, a remark-ably easy guest. While Desmond worked in his shed, he spent contented hours either curled in the shade reading a book or wandering the paths around the marshes and reed beds that surrounded the cottage, armed with a little magnifying jar and a pocket guide to insects. He had no allergies or irritating dietary fads but politely ate whatever food Desmond set before him.

An unobtrusive boy, he repeatedly put Desmond in mind of a characteristically mordant phrase of his mother's: *too good to live*. Desmond would miss him when he was gone and wondered if it would be thought sinister if he invited him back at the tired end of the summer holidays. Unmarried men had to be so careful around children these days and the precautions had a way of arousing, unbidden, thoughts of the very deeds they were designed to prevent. Hamish's mother could always be invited too, of course, but, being an adult, she required active hospitality whereas the boy required as little attention as a demurely self-contained whippet. Until now, that was.

The music had come to an end and there was no sound but the usual soughing of the night breeze in the reed beds and the persistent tapping of insects against the windowpane nearest to his lamp. Hamish's slightly hoarse, unbroken voice was so unexpected in the studious gloom that Desmond sloshed his drink on the upholstery in surprise.

'She's back,' Hamish told him. 'She wants to take me with her.'

232

'Jesus!' Desmond shouted. The child's mother had not breathed a word of this neurotic fear of his. Perhaps it was put on? A piece of manipulation born of resentment at her self-absorbed absence?

Hamish lingered on the edge of the pool of light and Desmond remembered his fear of the bedside light upstairs. Curious child! The boy's plump lower lip was trembling and he shivered. He had come down without his dressing gown and slippers and even in July the house was prone to draughts.

'Come on,' Desmond told him. 'Come and sit on the sofa and tell me all about the bloody woman.'

Hamish climbed obediently onto the chaise-longue, tucking his legs up beside him as though afraid of what might lurk underneath.

Feeling a great upswell of emotion, an unfamiliar mix of ordinary compassion and intense, heart-warming awareness of himself as a fatherly protector, Desmond unfurled an antique patchwork quilt he kept on one of the sofa arms for the bitterest nights and tucked it around him. 'There!' he said. 'That's better.'

The boy nodded, still wretchedly wan.

'Cup of cocoa? I can make some for us both.'

'No!' Hamish almost shouted, adding softly with tragic politeness, 'Please don't leave me, Desmond.'

'I won't. Good Lord! We didn't eat *so* much cheese with supper, did we?' Desmond sat back in his armchair, abandoning *The Global Village* for the time being. Perhaps the child felt the lack of a father. 'Tell me about it,' he said. 'Sometimes you have to talk about bad dreams to make them stay away.'

'She's not a dream.'

'But . . . Very well. If you say so. Who is she?'

'I *told* you. The Moth Lady. She's very thin and sort of . . . *whispery*. She's naked and she has compound eyes and antennae like brown feathers. She doesn't speak but she just uncoils her proboscis and touches me and I sort of *feel* her words. She wants to take me and I don't want to go.'

'Well you won't. You'll stay right here with me.'

'Please don't laugh at me.'

'Sorry. I wouldn't dream of it. Why does she want you?'

'I can't tell. But she wants to wrap me in a leathery cocoon so I can't move.'

'So you'll become a moth too?'

'No. For . . . I think it's for food.'

Desmond sighed. The boy had obviously spent far too long hunting dragonfly in the glare of noon. Perhaps he even had a touch of sunstroke. Desmond put a hand to Hamish's forehead but it was cool and slightly clammy. 'No one is taking you for food or for anything else,' he assured him. 'You curl up there and go to sleep. You're quite safe. If the Moth Lady or anyone else comes for you, I'll spray them with poison and stick them with a pin for you to

234

admire in the morning. There there. Only joking. Don't take on. You're sure no cocoa?'

'No, thank you. Desmond I . . . I think I'll be safe here. Won't I?'

'Absolutely.'

'Are all the windows closed?'

They weren't, of course, because it was July and the house would have swiftly become stuffy. His practice was to leave the dining room's window open and its door closed so that cooler air could be drawn in but no insects could see his reading light to be drawn in too.

'You know,' Desmond began, making one last appeal to reason. 'Moths do no harm to anything. It's only their caterpillars that eat wool or plants. I've given up planting verbascums because of the verbascum moth caterpillars and I never waste money on cashmere in case a clothes moth lays eggs on it, but I couldn't say I'd ever been *hurt* by one. Wasps and hornets, now, they're another matter. And there's a spider you find on compost heaps – the woodlouse spider – that can give you a painful nip . . .'

'I didn't say she was a moth. She's just *like* one.'

'Ah.'

Hamish was unconvinced but he was also exhausted, worn out by fear, and he yawned heavily as he spoke and pulled the quilt more snugly about him.

Relieved, imagining he would carry him back to bed when he himself retired, Desmond took a sip of what remained unspilled of his whisky and picked up the journal again. He found his brother's article once more. *The Global Village*, he read, *Towards a Dialectic*, but his concentration strayed within seconds and he soon realized he had read the same dull sentence several times over without even grasping the sense within its woolly construction.

He glanced up. The Schumann had ended and Hamish was sound asleep. Desmond discarded the journal again and reached instead for the little insect book that had inspired the boy's imagination so drastically. *232 Species in Colour*, it promised. He flicked past pages of beetles and flies of improbable size and came to a halt at a page devoted to the Goat Moth. Its body was elegantly striped in shades of grey and cream, it had, indeed, a certain dustily feminine elegance, but it was scarcely threatening even when reproduced to seem the size of his thumb. *Evil-looking caterpillar*, he read. *Has a pungent odour. Not easy to find as they feed on dead willow trees but a large tree will sometimes have hundreds of larvae boring in it.'*

There were several dead or dying willows across the way on the marsh's edge. He had a clear image of them as he too fell asleep; he pictured the unnerving way they had of seeming to rot and die, only to spring up again from where a broken limb had rooted in the mud.

He woke at the sound of his whisky glass smashing on the floor. He opened his eyes. There was a filthy smell coming from nearby, far more pungent than the smell of whisky. He traced it in seconds to the lamp where he saw, to his disgust, that some kind of fly or moth was cremating itself against the bulb. He turned the lamp off instinctively then cried out as broken glass pierced his sock. He limped across to the hall in the moonlight and turned on the light out there.

Hamish had taken himself off to bed. The quilt was discarded on the floor, with uncharacteristic carelessness.

Desmond tutted, folded it back onto the sofa arm, then swept the broken glass into a dustpan. He opened the back door to tip the shards directly into the rubbish bin and was briefly transfixed by the beauty of the night and took a few steps away from the door in his socks.

The breeze that had been stirring the reeds earlier was now quite gone so the air was full of suggestive scents – river mud, grass mowings, lavender from the bushes that defined the path to the garden gate and something else, something sweet. The full moon was still up, reflected in the water and silvering the reeds and willows.

Then he saw the moths. He saw only a few at

first, which were apparently crossing the garden from the marsh, but, tracing their flight, he saw that there were scores of them, maybe more than a hundred, dancing in the moonlight and seeming to gather about Hamish's unlit, reopened window.

He ran back through the house, ignoring the pain in his cut foot, shouting the boy's name.

The bed was empty, the sheets quite cold. An old, long-forgotten fear told him, as he ran from room to empty room, that his search would be fruitless.

He had waded, gasping, around the marsh's fringes for half an hour, muddying his boots and trousers, before he thought to ring the police and the boy's mother.

He knew what people would say. He knew how it would look.

FREEDOM

Lorna's formidable sister-in-law went caravanning every summer and was a keen member of the Caravan Club and observer of its clannish codes. She and her husband always stayed in well-populated camp-sites, usually by prior arrangement with fellow members. They would arrange their caravans in a tight formation – pioneer style – to keep the rougher, tented element at bay, and would recreate a suburb on wheels, visiting one another's caravans for drinks and bridge and ingenious one-pot suppers.

If Lorna had not sensed this was not for her, the sister-in-law confirmed it by never once urging her and her family to follow suit and join in the fun. She handed round photographs of the holidays and explained the features of each restlessly upgraded caravan with the patronizing air of a displaced urbanite explaining running water and regular bath-times to a barefoot family in a mud hut: expecting wide-eyed admiration, not company amidst the bubbles.

Lorna and her husband preferred to rent remote cottages for their holidays. These were invariably more basically equipped than the sister-in-law's latest caravan and were found in the trustworthy back pages of *The Lady*. Holidays were exhausting for Lorna because she had to pack most of her kitchen equipment and larder as well as pillows and bedding, cats and dogs, maps and library books, but it was precisely because each holiday was a bit like moving house that it was so stimulating. Lumpy beds, idio-syncratic plumbing and other people's taste were half the adventure. Adapting to new surroundings stirred one up and refreshed one's appreciation of home. Then there was the matter of space. The sister-in-law had just two very good if unenquiring children who were easily pleased whereas it was a point of reassurance for Lorna that her three boys and a baby were restless and inquisitive and not easily to be contained in a mobile home, however well equipped.

But that morning she was detained at the village garage while Mr Boorman topped up the oil and water for her and, idly inspecting the huddle of second-hand cars on his little forecourt, she came across the caravan. It was eight years old, so must have been made in nineteen fifty-something and was called The Sprite, which charmed her. It was powder-blue and cream on the outside and seemed to have more character than the new, white things the sister-in-law favoured. She opened the narrow door and stepped up inside.

It was tiny but ingenious. There were two beds, both doubling as seats, a little Formica-topped table, a cold-box, a sink and a two-ring gas cooker. There were curtains whose gay fabric reminded her of a favourite skirt she had worn out before her marriage and the cushions were covered with a sensible sort of orangey bouclé. She sat at the table, gazing around her and out of the little windows, and was won over.

One could be sure Mr Boorman had maintained it well – he was quite misty-eyed about selling it – and the price he was asking was not much more than two months' rent on their usual sort of cottage. She impulsively wrote a cheque for a deposit then set about persuading her husband over Irish stew that evening.

He was unsettled at first and seemed doubtful of the taste of her suggestion – he had never approved of his brother's marriage or his subsequent cara-vanning – but she won him over by appealing to his frugality. This would be like a cottage where two months' rent lasted for years! They could travel far further than usual, she suggested, by being able to spend a night here and a night there. They could journey the length of the country. They could show the children castles and cathedrals and Hadrian's Wall. They didn't even have to stay in horrid camp-sites every night if they didn't mind washing with a flannel or making do with the sea. They could buy a tent as an overflow dorm for the older boys. It would be fun. It would be an adventure.

And since he had always trusted her to arrange everything and was too busy to be bothered with it himself, he agreed.

What she didn't realize and certainly didn't admit to herself until years later, was that what had charmed her about The Sprite was its suggestion of precious freedom. It had reminded her, she saw too late, of Wendy Houses where she had made pretend tea and raised pretend families as a girl. The escape she had pictured in it, beside a dreamy loch or over-looking a romantic ruin, was made on her own.

Her husband was a clumsily erratic driver – he had learnt on a tank during the war – and had no more training than she did in how to reverse a trailer still less a view-obscuring caravan. Following religi-ously a circular itinerary supplied by the AA, they journeyed all the way to Northumberland and back but it was a white-knuckle ride. He kept forgetting the caravan was there, so it was forever mounting pavements and scattering pedestrians. They were twice cautioned by ashen-faced policemen and had a very nasty row with a woman who claimed they had scraped the paintwork on her roadside bungalow. It was a miracle nobody was killed.

The children loved the caravan at first but never mastered their disappointment at not being allowed to ride in it. They saw castles and abbeys galore and completed well-stuffed holiday diaries but the weather was filthy, the boys never got the hang of putting up their tent unassisted, the baby cried for England, they all caught nastily productive colds and the one night they stayed in a camp-site smart enough to have passed muster with the sister-in-law, the Jack Russell disgraced them all by proudly rounding up a flock of sheep and driving it among the furious campers. Lorna was a cook who needed space, she discovered, and cooking family-sized meals on a doll-sized stove proved such a strain they repeatedly dined on fish and chips or even pork pies.

The only one who really enjoyed the experience was her husband, who was a natural Spartan and never happier than when doing without or making do. When Lorna's camera film was posted back from the developer's in its distinctive yellow envelope, she found that he was smiling in every photograph, pipe clenched in chattering teeth.

A few weeks after their return, with the excuse that it took up too much room in their drive, Lorna hitched up The Sprite one more time and drove it to her parents' house on the Isle of Wight.

'Easy enough to collect when we need it again,' she said but somehow the occasion never arose.

Shown the holiday photographs, in particular one with the baby parked morosely on its potty and Lorna furiously frying sausages beneath a line of flapping nappies, the sister-in-law pronounced them the sort of people who gave caravanning a bad name.

⁖

They had a field beyond the garden wall, Lily's field, bought with Lily's money to stop anyone building on it and where she kept a pair of retired donkeys to hold the thistles in check. What with the cost of maintaining fences and paying vet's bills – donkeys not being as hardy as they looked – the field had become her folly. So there was a certain irony in parking the daughter's folly within the mother's.

Lily cursed the caravan at first, thinking it a senseless, common creation, unable to imagine why Lorna had bought the thing or why, having seen sense, she kept it. Then weeds grew about its wheels and she began to overlook it.

Influenced by advertising, she had always looked forward to her husband's retirement, picturing it as one long summer weekend. She should have realized that weekends were only a pleasure because they were short and exceptional. There was a limit to how often he could clip the hedges or mow the lawn. His hobby had always been bonsai and that was scarcely time-consuming. Now that he was home all the time, he was bored, and now he was no longer earning, he was niggardly.

She loved him dearly, of course, but theirs had always been a combative love founded, she now saw, on her clawing back in the course of the working week the territory she conceded at weekends. Now that he no longer had work, he began to take an invasive interest in hers, finding ways of cooking and cleaning that were somehow superior. Their garden was large but the house wasn't and with him home all the time she found his temper and restless energy left less and less space for her.

One autumn afternoon, when he elected to make large quantities of admirably cheap jam from the bullaces that thrived along a nearby bridleway, she realized she was on the verge of losing her temper and saying something she might regret. So she stalked out to commune with the donkeys in the drizzle. Their stoicism, and the meaty sensation of their ears beneath her hands, were usually calming but that day they were being wilfully unsociable. Then the drizzle turned without warning to a downpour so she claimed the nearest available shelter.

It was musty but it was dry, and she perceived as she sat on one of the squashy little banquettes, miraculously peaceful compared to the house. The drizzle turned to full throttle rain and Lily was startled by the noise it made on the skylight. Stranded but curious, she investigated further. Lorna was a reliably bad housekeeper and, sure enough, had not thought to empty the cupboards entirely. Lily found a packet of gypsy creams, Lapsang tea and a bag of sultanas. She experimented with the little stove and found there was still gas in the canister and water in the whistling kettle. Hunting for matches, she found some overdue library books, including a smutty American crime novel. She set the kettle to boil, discovered that a tug of a leather strap turned the larger banquette into a fairly comfortable double bed with a charming view of her donkeys sheltered under distant trees and settled down with a lapful of sultanas and the biscuit packet tucked in the crook of her arm and began to read.

This might have remained an isolated incident had bullace pickle not become the next day's project and the stench of spice and vinegar not driven her outside again.

She finished the crime novel and started another. She brought out fresh water and better biscuits, secretly purchased. By stealthy degrees the caravan became hers. She bought second-hand paperbacks for its bookshelf, a little radio, a cheery pelargonium, a doormat. Claiming her GP had told her to exercise more, she took to embarking on daily walks which led circuitously to its door and an hour or two of cherished, feminine peace. She didn't care that it was a little shabby and dated: the Doris Day décor was a reminder of happier, earlier years in her marriage. She didn't care that her husband took advantage of her absences to drink. When they met up again at teatime, each was as sweet as pie.

☙

Leo inherited the field from his mother who in turn had inherited it from hers. It was months before he visited in person, then he drove over with a bossy boyfriend who was determined they should build eco-friendly holiday chalets on it. No one had mentioned the caravan, which had been broken into and vandalized as much by time and weather as by disaffected local youth. While the bossy boyfriend measured and photographed the site and took notes, Leo let himself in and sat, astonished, on the only surviving cushion.

He had no memories of his holiday in it as a baby but had spent days and nights in there as a child because his grandfather couldn't bear small boys in the house and banished Leo and his brothers to the field on visits. His grandparents' marriage was not happy – his grandfather drank and his grandmother probably did too in order to cope with his temper. Looking back, he suspected she used to hide in the caravan when they weren't visiting. Quite possibly she resented their visits for depriving her of a bolt-hole, but perhaps she sheltered behind the business of entertaining guests as effectively as she could in a field at the bottom of a long garden.

Being noisily insecure, Leo's brothers had forever found excuses to cross the field and garden to visit the adults at nights but Leo had loved the caravan, loved the sensation it offered of playing house and the feral, male air it acquired after a few days of their presence in it.

The same fifties curtains swung in the breeze now, sun-bleached but intact. The bumpy fabric his fingers remembered still covered the cushion and on the shelf, dog-eared and buckled by alternating damp and heat, he found the collection of unsuitable novels he had learned to decipher and relish over a succession of half-terms.

He took up *Death Becomes Her*, flicked the mouse droppings off it, opened it at random then thrust his nose between the pages and took a luxurious sniff from its spine. The strangely mixed bouquet was unchanged and unmistakable: glue, camping gas, sunshine. Freedom.

He looked up to find the boyfriend staring from the doorway.

'You wouldn't understand,' he told him. 'It's a caravan thing.'

GENTLEMAN'S RELISH

In his more desolate periods, Frank told himself the boys had grown up without him. He saw them on Sundays if they had no other plans and on holidays but otherwise his sons were shadowy presences in his life. They were largely represented to him by things: clothes discarded on chair backs, boots tumbled on the doormat, the detritus of midnight snacks encountered as he snatched his breakfast.

On weekdays he left the house before they appeared, so as to catch an early commuter train into town to his job in the City. When they were younger he used to walk around the bedrooms waking them before he left. He had treasured this brief, one-sided contact, the glimpses of them still capable of childish vulnerability in sleep. However a casually cruel hint was dropped that a clock radio was a less startling way to start the day so now he made do with taking his wife up her breakfast tray, deprived of precious contact with the others.

The eldest was at university now, the middle one, the rebel, had left school early to take a well-paid, unsuitable job and had developed a mysterious social life and with it, an aversion to eating any meal with his parents. The youngest, at fourteen, was effectively a bed and breakfast guest, for he ate his supper with the boarders at school. He was required to stay on there for prep, which took until nine, and often elected to stay on longer to play with his house string quartet. He was rarely home before ten-thirty, by which time Frank had invariably fallen asleep in front of the television, so missed him.

The weekends were thus a rare chance to encounter one another. Conditioned as he was to waking early, it was small hardship to take only one extra hour in bed so as to come downstairs in time to see a bit of his youngest over breakfast.

An only child of a widowed father, Frank had been raised by people paid to raise him. Looking about him as a teenager he had been led to assume that marriage was life's great pleasure, fatherhood its dutiful cost and so was overwhelmed to find that in reality the emphases were reversed. He loved his wife well enough but it was his children he adored. Bathing them, playing with them, teaching them to read, catch a ball, build a sandcastle, gave him more pleasure than a man was expected to reveal. In the long hours in which he was forced out of his sons' company, he worried about them and dreamed of the simple, physical pleasure of their presence with the mind-addling intensity of new love.

It was a shock to realize that with each boy in turn, the cruel necessity of Frank's day-long absences in town weighed against their mother's constant surveillance to make him almost a stranger to them, an orderly intruder on their raucous nursery joys. Made to feel shy among his own, he found he could show less and less of what he felt.

The onset of puberty rendered each boy in turn a stranger to his father. The first two morphed from child to young adult in a kind of frenzy of bad temper, worse skin and withering – if inarticulate – contempt. The youngest should by now have embarked on this necessarily painful phase, burning off his sweetness to acquire strength, but seemed to be holding the process at bay. His voice had broken and he was shaving occasionally: there was nothing wrong hormonally. As the family's Benjamin he was the one they least wanted to see leave boyhood behind. At times he seemed to share this reluctance. At others it was as though the habitual dreaminess of his childhood had subtly turned to a sly watchfulness. Thanks to his brothers he had twice watched at first hand the process by which boy turned man; he was an expert.

They didn't talk much at these Saturday breakfasts. Like his mother, the boy usually ate with his nose in a book. Frank refused to be put off, however, and would make a point of asking him how he was progressing at school, how the house teams were doing, that sort of thing. An inoffensive line of enquiry. He would like to have heard answers to real questions, of course. *Are you as happy as you seem? Do you think about sex all the time? Or love, even? Is anything worrying you?* All the questions his own father never asked him. But to get such answers one had to elicit them and precisely because his father had never asked him such things he had neither language nor courage to ask them of the boy. So they would speak instead in the traditional coded idiom of fathers and sons wherein safe questions of sport and work stood in for more risky ones of happiness and affection.

Once she was up and dressed, his wife talked almost incessantly, maintaining the sort of amiable flow she had been raised to believe was required of women to fill the awkward silences left by males. When she was present, all conversation passed through her as though she alone could bridge the linguistic gulfs between man and man or generation and generation. But all they heard of her on these early Saturday mornings were the murmur of her bedside radio and the occasional clink of her breakfast china.

Today was not as other Saturdays. Today Frank would have to speak to the boy without code because yesterday he had received a rare phone call at the office from his housemaster. Startled from the pleasant afternoon trance brought on by cross-word defeat, an excess of dull memos, and a fulsome retirement lunch in the boardroom, Frank's immedi-ate reaction was nauseous fear. The only possible reason for such a call was a clumsy, accidental death. In the seconds it took his secretary to put the call through, he had pictured the boy with his neck broken on the gym's parquet floor or floating in a crimson bloom beneath a diving board. Then he heard embarrassment rather than fear in the other man's tone and relaxed a little. The crisis was of a stealthier kind than he had first imagined.

With similar backgrounds – Classics, army, early motherlessness – the two men shared a difficulty in approaching emotive subjects head on but, with a few minutes of coughing, nervous chuckles and sucking on pipes, had established that the boy had written an inappropriate communication to one of the younger French teachers who, luckily, had panicked and passed it on to the housemaster. The words *love letter* had not been spoken but Frank had deciphered them in the man's pained, unfinished sentences and slightly wild references to *hothouse emotions* and the need to encourage more healthy interaction with the local girls' school. There was talk of a mixed-sex debating society or drama club.

'Of course, it's entirely up to you,' the housemaster had said. 'If you'd rather we left this in your hands we can. Or I can pass it on to the chaplain. Good man. Experienced at dealing with this sort of thing. Discreet. Queerly enough, he has a background in industrial relations.'

Ashamed that it should be assumed he would pass the buck at once, Frank startled himself by saying that no, he would handle the matter himself and attempt a fatherly conversation. The thought of this had stayed with him through the afternoon, as insistent as indigestion. The need for honourable secrecy had introduced an unpleasant whiff of deceit to the evening's conversation with his wife. The air needed clearing.

'Morning.'

'Morning, Dad.'

The boy was eating muesli and chopped banana, nose deep in a small book of French poetry. It took Frank a while to fetch his habitual breakfast things from kitchen to breakfast room. He half hoped he would take too long over it and let the boy slip away.

'Coffee?' he called through.

'It's okay, Dad. I've got a cup. Thanks.'

During the week, Frank knew, the boy and the middle brother had established a touchingly manly routine whereby they took their breakfast on either side of the wall, one at the breakfast room table, one in the kitchen, so that, while forced to rise at the same hour, neither needed actually to speak.

At last he sat across from him, a reassuring library thriller wedged open beside him with a pot of Gentleman's Relish, and began to butter toast. The boy sighed and turned a page. His nails were too neat and too clean, as was his hair. This was a different breed of rebelliousness to the more usual sort shown by his brothers at this age and correspondingly harder to meet with equanimity. Frank suffered vivid nightmares sometimes, in which the boy developed a bright-eyed religious mania and took to paying evangelical calls on all their friends in a suit and tie or took to entertaining middle-aged women to tea and petits fours. Lank hair or a filthy leather jacket would have been almost reassuring.

At moments like this, aware that he was imposing himself on the periphery of the boy's small circle of wordless restraint, Frank remembered the profound physical disgust his own father engendered in him at this age, particularly in the queasy early hours of the day. The muffled clicking of his false teeth as he chewed bacon, the sickly spiced smell of the lotion on his hair or merely the inoffensive sound of him folding his newspaper had made Frank want to flee the room to an untainted atmosphere. Usually he recalled this at the worst moments, as he was crunching cold toast or gulping coffee and nearly choked in his effort to be as un-repulsive as possible. Even as he checked himself, he knew it was hopeless; the werewolf-sharp senses of adolescence would pick out a patch of bristles his razor had missed or latch on with revulsion to the pinging sound his teaspoon made on his mug.

'Heavy day today?' he asked, refusing to let the slim volume of Rimbaud put him off.

The boy sighed again, pushed aside his cereal bowl and tore into a tangerine. His eyes retained their sleepy focus on the pages of his book. 'Not really. The usual. Double Latin with a prose. French. History.'

'But it's a half day, yes?'

'Saturdays always are, Dad.'

'Of course.'

'Fives match this afternoon, then *Elijah* at Glee Club then supper then prep then Compline then home.' The boy was humouring him as one might a tedious aunt.

A small, feminine cough came from upstairs. It was as though, even at long range, his wife could tell their conversation lacked sparkle.

'No cello tonight, then? No quartet?'

'Not on a Saturday.'

Desperate, Frank glanced at his son's book for a cue and asked without thinking, 'So who's your French master this year?'

'Mr Lawrence. Tony Lawrence.' The boy cleared his throat and fiddled with the tangerine peel.

He shut the book, dared to meet his father's eye. 'He's just come down from Oxford. I think he's only passing through. The other boys tease him a bit.' Running out of words to mumble, he blushed intensely and dropped his gaze back to the book.

Frank was appalled. He had not meant to be so direct. He had planned a circuitous approach with questions about friends in general and then on to friendly teachers and the folly of favouritism. 'But you get on with French, don't you?' he asked. 'You want to carry on with it for your As, your mother said.'

'Yeah, Dad. Look. I should go and brush my teeth.'

He slipped away, leaving the poetry book behind in his confusion. Rimbaud's photograph stared out from the cover. He looked petulant, probably unwashed, full of churning, filthy thoughts epigrammatically expressed; a toxic Peter Pan.

Frank stared back as he ate his toast. Out of the blue he remembered the fuss when his father caught him reading the charlady's copy of *Forever Amber*. Confirmation classes had been brought forward by several months and there had been a sequence of enforced excursions with hearty boys who were not quite friends.

He heard taps turned on and off, a lavatory flush. There was a brief flurry of easy chat as the boy called in to sit at the foot of his mother's bed then the thunder of his feet on the stairs.

'You forgot this,' Frank called out.

The boy glanced into the breakfast room, his pallor restored, bringing with him a faint whiff of the blue chemical he used to keep spots at bay. He glanced at the book carelessly.

'Oh, that. I'm just reading that for fun. Have a good day. See you later.'

'Bye.'

And he was gone. There came a crunch of cycle wheels on gravel, the desolate clang of the iron garden gate.

Frank rang the housemaster quickly, closing an intervening door so his wife should not hear.

'I think, on reflection, perhaps a chat with the chaplain's our best option,' he told him. 'Unless you think . . .?'

'Er no. Quite,' the housemaster said. 'I'll have a word this morning. He's a good man.'

'Discreet, you said. Not sure my wife should . . .'

'Absolutely.'

Hanging up, he felt the relief of a burden lifted and soon after, the less familiar sensation of guilt at a responsibility shirked.

He washed the last traces of Gentleman's Relish off his knife then climbed the stairs to fetch his wife's tray. He would spend the morning sterilizing seed trays and scrubbing flower pots in icy water as a penance.

AUTHOR'S NOTE

Several of these stories have made earlier appearances, often in slightly different forms. *Gentleman's Relish* was commissioned by Radio 4 for a week of stories focusing on fathers and sons, *Freedom* for one marking the hundredth birthday of the Caravan Club and *Fourth of July, 1862* to celebrate the anniversary of the publication of *Alice in Wonderland*, *Making Hay* for a sequence of broadcasts from the Hay Festival and *The Lesson* for a series on the theme of prison. (In a culture cruelly short of regular outlets for short fiction, Radio 4's precious, if tiny, slots at weekday teatimes more than justify the BBC licence fee . . .) Both *The Dark Cutter* and *Petals on a Pool* were commissioned by *Asia Literary Review* while *Cookery* and *The Excursion* were commissioned by Peter Burton for his anthologies, *The Mammoth Book of Gay Short Stories* and *Death Comes Easy*. *Saving Space* and *Brahms and Moonshine* first appeared in *Endellion Notes*, the organ of the St Endellion Music Festivals.